D1321983

The Travels of Ibn Fudayl

George R. Sole is an English explorer, traveller and a
translator who has spent a considerable time in the
MENA region. After graduating from the University
of Oxford's Balliol College with a First Class honours in 1961,
he spent ten years under the service of the Sultan of Oman
fighting the Communist insurgency. After an incident where
he released a greased piglet into a ballroom of diplomats he was
dishonourably discharged by the British Army having sparked
a diplomatic incident described by one ambassador as being 'as
catastrophic as the British army deciding to use animal grease
for their cartridges in India before the mutiny in 1857'. Out of
money and without any connections unlike his contemporaries,
he resorted to exploring the Empty Quarter in Arabia with
his irresolute fixer of unknown provenance, Abu Hanzala ibn
al-Haram ibn al-Halal, from the Banu Kilab tribe known for
being great carrion eaters. In these travels he came across many
Yemeni tribesman who persuaded him to search for the famed
city of Ubar - the Atlantis of the Sands. He gave up his search
after Sir Ranulph Fiennes pipped him. Defeated and dejected,
Mr R. Sole parted from Abu Hanzala and dedicated himself to
his Arabic studies in Cairo and now resides in Amman where
he translates numerous obscure translations of Arabic travellers
and historians making them available to the wider public.

GEORGE R. SOLE

The Travels of Ibn Fudayl

DARF PUBLISHERS
LONDON

Published by Darf Publishers 2017

Darf Publishers Ltd
277 West End Lane
West Hampstead
London
NW6 1QS

The Travels of Ibn Fudayl
By George R. Sole

The moral right of the author has been asserted

Cover designed by Chris Wren

Printed and bound in Great Britain by Clays Ltd, St Ives plc

ISBN-13: 978-1-85077-303-0
eBook ISBN: 978-1-85077-304-7

This novel's story and characters are fictitious. For dramatic, contextual and
narrative purposes, certain real authors, scholars, historical figures and religious
events are mentioned throughout. The reader must acknowledge that these are
used in a fictional context to satirise the pretentious world of academia, and in
no way is done to besmirch their good character, ability or intentions.

www.darfpublishers.co.uk

Acknowledgements

The author would like to thank the wonderful assistance that scholars at the School of African and Oriental Studies (SOAS) have provided, especially the noteworthy Oriental scholars Dr Hamza Malik and Dr Taheer Said for their wonderful discussions on the problems of translating. Dr Abdul Mu'min Hussain for his unlimited help on the difficult philosophical questions that the book offers. The assistance provided by Professor Imad Ahmad of Keble College, Oxford for his linguistic expertise and allowing the author to vent his frustrations at this most difficult text. The author is grateful to the Medieval Scholar Dr T. S. Asbridge of Queen Mary and Westfield College, who introduced him to this rich field of historiography. Professor Kevyn Lenfest of John Hopkins for providing helpful suggestions to the text and political analysis. The author would also like to thank the unrelenting constructive criticism provided by Dr Caterina Pinto, Dr Vittoria Volgare and Dr Valentina Viene from The School of Oriental Studies in Naples. Finally, the author would like to thank his family and the numerous friends for their belief and support for such a trying endeavour.

(Damascus, April 1, 2007)

Introduction

On 19th of April 711, the seventeen-year-old Tariq bin Ziyad led his seven thousand Arab and Berber troops across the straits of Gibraltar that still bears his name.[1] Tariq, ordered by the Umayyad caliph, invited by the Byzantine exarch of Septer and supported by a flotilla of Count Julian, a Visigoth noble, made the landing. Once onshore, he burnt his boats rallying his seven thousand by his dream that the Prophet Muhammad had come to him and promised him the land: the only way was either victory or martyrdom. His army completely routed the thirty thousand Visigothic troops and confined them to a small strip of land in the north of the Iberian Peninsula.

The victory inaugurated seven hundred years of Muslim rule in Iberia. At one point controlling Barcelona and penetrating deep into France; only to be stopped by Charles Martel at the battle of Poitiers in 732. It is a great irony then, that on 19th of April 2006, the only extant manuscript of this book should have been discovered, quite by chance, by a filing clerk at the Asad library, Damascus. *The Travels of Ibn Fudayl*, as it has become known, expresses vividly the magnificence of a world now gone. This translation gives a remarkable picture

---

[1]   Jebel Tariq means the mountain of Tariq.

of Andalusia that will interest both the curious reader as well as the specialist.[2]

Abu Ayyub bin Fudayl (d. 1196) follows in the same traditions as other Muslim travellers and geographers. The manuscript suggests that, before settling in Syria, Ibn Fudayl had visited India, Persia, and the Levant. As for his life, he has been mentioned by other scholars of the time in passing. Some labelled him as a zindiq,[3] a freethinker, others considered him as part of a Sufi order mixing the Neo-platonic thought of Plotinus with the esoteric mysticism of the Shi'ites. There are also lines of poetry that have been attributed to him but they cannot be verified with enough certainty. For example:

> *I am the existent and yet the non-existent,*
> *I am the ocean that fits in a drinker's cup.*
> *Questions that you hold to be self-evident,*
> *With my being I knock and open up.*[4]

What we can surmise from his works is that he was undoubtedly a polymath: a student, a scholar of considerable ability, an able poet and an eloquent speaker with a remarkable inquisitiveness that infected all that read him. We know that he was a native of Fatimid Cairo, or Fustat as it was then known. This incomplete

---

[2]   From that day on, the provinces ruled by the Muslims came to be known as Andalusia. A name, according to some chroniclers, derived from the Vandals that once inhabited the land. The Christian part remained under its Latin name: Hispania or Spania.

[3]   Atheist or freethinker, word is of Persian origin.

[4]   P189, *Al-Wadih fee balagha*, Muhammad Ashraf Ali, Calcutta, (1896).

work, *Min As-Sabil ad-Dalla ila Sabeel al-Haq* or 'From the Misguided Path to the Path of Truth', reveals all these aspects of the man.

It becomes apparent that Ibn Fudayl was someone imbued with the tradition for exploration. Although Ibn Fudayl does not appear to be particularly religious, as is the case with Ibn Jubayr, in some ways he was the very manifestation of the Quranic injunction on the Faithful: to travel the Earth and see what has passed. Despite not being overtly Islamic like Abu Hanifa, Ahmad bin Hanbal, al-Ghazzali or Ibn Arabi, yet just like Ibn Sina, Ibn Bajjah, Uthman bin Fathun, Ahmad bin Majriti (d.1008) and Ibn Rushd, he was an expression and product of Islamic civilisation. In his own little way, Ibn Fudayl articulated the confidence and curiosity of the Islamic civilisation; a civilisation that was willing to explore new frontiers unafraid to open up new doors for material, intellectual and spiritual benefit. Thus, it is not surprising that the period between the 7th to 15th centuries saw remarkable inroads into these fields.

The literature of the age reveals numerous accounts of similar men. Ibn Fadlan and Ibn Rustuh al-Isfahani gave an account of the Rus, Ibn Jubayr of the Arabian Peninsula, Ibn Battuta of China and India, al-Maqdisi and Usama bin Munqidh the Franks and the maps of al-Idrisi that Columbus used for his journeys, all display a healthy curiosity of the world that surrounded them. These fruitful periods were peppered with names of people that contributed to science, medicine, philosophy and geography that has shaped the modern world as we know it. In particular Andalusia, although this far-flung region remained at the periphery of the Islamic world and was no comparison to the great centres of Islamicate

as was the case with Damascus and Baghdad; the role it played in
relation to the West, as a medium for knowledge, is unmeasurable.
Andalusia played a great function in transmitting scholarship,
science, art and culture to Europe. It was the genesis or, to say
the least, contributed greatly to the European Renaissance. The
reader must not forget, however, that this intellectual exchange is
quite natural in human history. Just like presently the Occident
serves as the transmitter of learning to the Orient. Likewise, when
the Occident was experiencing its darkest age, the Orient was
experiencing its golden. The result was osmosis.

What makes Ibn Fudayl so useful is that he gives a very
detailed account of the life and mores of Andalusian society.
He recalls the trends and currents that influenced this society
in flux, in a way that no other contemporary had done in the
period of the Party Kings, *'asr al-Muluk at-Tawai'f*. That is not
to say we do not have information about Andalusia in general.
In fact, there is a plethora of information, through the likes of
Abdullah bin Bullugin, the road books or *masalik* of al-Ya'qubi,
Ibn al-Fakih and Ibn Rata, Ahmad Razi (d.955), al-Istakhri
(d.935), his contemporary al-Hawkal, Ibn Hazm, as well as
secondary materials from al-Maqdisi and al-Idrisi. But none can
give such an impersonal and philosophical explanation of the
events witnessed. Not at least until the arrival of Ibn Khaldun
in the 15th century. Ibn Fudayl's unique contribution makes his
work so valuable to the historian. It is so rich in detail that the
reader feels he is almost living with the author.

When Ibn Fudayl arrived in Andalusia, the reader is not aware
that Andalusia was not what it was. The history of Andalusia up
to the arrival of Ibn Fudayl can be divided into four stages.

Stage one, from 711 to 929. The region was ruled by a number of emirs who vied with one another for power. Andalusia was experiencing the birth pangs of a foundling state whereby the various parties competed with each other for control. The massacre of the Umayyad dynasty by the Abbasids in 756 meant that the last surviving descendant of the Umayyad dynasty, Abd ar-Rahman ad-Dakhili, arrived in Andalusia and successfully subdued the divergent groups and established himself as the emir of Cordoba. The period was characterised with expansion and consolidation of power. His descendant, Abd ar-Rahman III, ascended the emirate in 912 and extended its power in North Africa and Andalusia.

Stage two, from 925 to 1009. In 925 Abd ar-Rahman III proclaimed himself caliph and turned the province into a caliphate. His need for legitimacy ushered in a profound cultural flowering for all the inhabitants of al-Andalus. Despite there being three caliphates - the Fatimid, the Abbasid and his own - the Umayyad caliphate survived the geopolitical strains that the rival caliphates threw at it. This was due to Umayyad Spain producing capable enough caliphs not only to manage and unite the Muslim population against the Christian kingdoms, confined to the north of the Iberian Peninsula, but also to check the ambitions of the rival caliphates. By the 10th century, Andalusia had become one of the greatest centres for philological, literary, and juridical culture. However, by 1086 this 'ornament of the world', as the Saxon Poetess Hroswitha called Andalusia, had fallen into deep division and ushered in the third stage: a period of weakness.

Stage three from 1009 to 1086. The weak period was due to the sagacious and able commander al-Mansur bin Abi Amir, the majordomo of the Umayyad caliph, who took over the administrative control of Umayyad Spain in 965. Although he maintained the protocols of the caliphate he had inadvertently, through his political machinations, weakened the caliphate. His military policies introduced to al-Andalus a large number of mercenaries of Berber origin who, after his death, served as a powerful bloc of agitation against the natives. After his death in 997, this bloc rose to greater prominence and demanded a greater role in the affairs of the peninsula. Consequently, Andalusia fell into a series of political struggles that split its unity and coherence that was the key to its strength. The civil war that ensued between 1009-1013 destroyed any semblance of Muslim unity; the caliphate floundered in 1031. Andalusia fell into a period of further weakness.

The differences of the various factions split the caliphate into various fragmented statelets, all vying with each other for supremacy. The irrevocable damage to the caliphate meant two things for Andalusia. One, it saw one of the greatest flowerings of culture as these 'petty kings' competed with each other for legitimacy and became patrons of the Arts. Two, they enlisted the aid of the Christian kingdoms who seized the opportunity to re-conquer their lost territories. The Christian kingdoms in effect, became arbiters of the disputes that occurred between Berbers who fought Slavs who, in their turn, fought Arabs and so on. These 'petty kings', as they were labelled, provided the impetus for the formation of the Christian ideology of *Reconquista,* which ultimately culminated in the fall of Nasrid Granada in 1492. However, at the peaceful but symbolic takeover of Toledo in 1085 by King Alfonso VI of Leon and Castile, the idea of *Reconquista* was still in its infancy. The ideology would not reach its full realization until perhaps after the fall of the Kingdom of Jerusalem in 1187. The fall of Toledo made the danger to Muslim Andalusia extremely apparent. The petty kingdoms saw no option but to seek help from North Africa. This led to the fourth stage.

Fourth stage, from 1086 to 1195, the period of foreign intervention in Andalusia. In 1086, to the nervous apprehension of many princes in al-Andalus, the Almoravid ruler of North Africa was invited to defend it from the ambitions of the Christian kingdoms. That same year the austere leader of the Almoravids, Yusuf bin Tashfin, crossed the straits and landed in Algeciras. He inflicted a severe defeat on the Christians at az-Zallaqa. By 1094 he had united the country, removed the somewhat decadent princes and annexed their states, installed his own governors, regained Valencia from the Christians and halted their advance. Al-Andalus had effectively become a vassal state to the Almoravids. However, the petty rivalries never quite went away between the governors or sultans who were invested with power to rule the land on behalf of the Almoravids. This was in fact the case with Sultan Abdullah bin Mardanish, the emir of the province of Valencia, who always sought to expand his power and influence through his patronage. Thus, despite the austere nature of Almoravid rule, with their patronage these emirs still attracted the finest minds in the Islamic world. It was precisely due to men such as Sultan Mardanish that Ibn Fudayl could find himself writing his amazing tract.

Finally, without dwelling too much on the problems of translation, a note on the text. Arabic is an extremely rich and subtle language. The act of translating into English sometimes results in the subtlety of meaning often becoming lost in translation; any deficiency therefore in the translation is borne wholly on my shoulders.

It is this very problem in translating that has meant that up to now *The Travels of Ibn Fudayl* has not been available to Western scholarship. It is hoped that with this major new translation, new inroads can be made for scholarship and research.

This translation has been carefully prepared by myself after having consulted and checked with major Orientalists in the field today, namely, the aforementioned professors at the School of African and Oriental studies and The School of Oriental Studies in Naples.

However, an annotated glossary has been added to equip the reader with keywords, for a full appreciation of the medieval manuscript. I was loath to add more footnotes to the translation, since it is already copiously annotated.

Let the reader be cautious in approaching these words, for in some ways they may appear as insults when, in actual fact, the dry tone suggests otherwise. Perhaps Ibn Fudayl did not view these words as insults at all and his scintillating mind may have thought of them with a certain degree of favour. Or his scientific mind recalled these words within the cold framework of reason, leaving all emotions aside.

Annotated Glossary

Kalb (pl. *kilab*) and *kulayb* (diminutive) - literally means dog. However, if it refers to Ibn Kalb, it means 'son of a dog' or sometimes it is translated, mistakenly in my opinion, as 'son of a bitch'. Arguably, it shows frightful ignorance of the translator when he fails to realise that Arab tribes often have names such as *Kilab*, (dogs) or *Asad* (lion) to denote the warlike nature of their respective tribe. Thus, when the reader comes across the word Ibn Kalb he needs to read it in context. In the case of a man calling an Egyptian taxi driver 'Ibn Kalb' in Cairo, as the latter has fleeced him for eighty euros, this translator would recommend that it should be understood as 'son of a bitch'.[5] With regards to *The Travels of Ibn Fudayl*, it should be taken in the context of Arab tribal mores.

---

[5] For further study see *Al-'Ilm al-Sadid fi Mufradat al-Kalb, The Accurate Science of the Synonyms of the Dog*, Dr Rabie bin al-Kalb bin al-Kulayb bin al-Kilaab bin al-Jahsh, Oxford (2001). The author wrote this text as a clarification from the ignorant Arabic teachers at his faculty who, instead of recognising Arabic tribal mores, understood his name in the wrong way and smirked every time he walked past. But what motivated him was actually more than just slighted honour, as the author says in the Introduction: 'I decided to write this book because one day, whilst teaching at the prestigious SOAS University, one of my students offered to cook me dinner in return for an increase in her marks. The delightful student, unlike those females in my country, did not know a thing about cooking and I sat on her rather messy bed and watched her

Jahsh (pl. *juhush*) literally means 'son of a wild donkey', a colt. Again, this can be taken literally, which depending on where you are could lead to fisticuffs. Or it could refer to tribal confederations in the Levant. The plural form *juhush* could also refer, as the ancient Arabic dictionaries have it, to 'a small fat boy'. Ibn Fudayl may have had a predilection to small fat boys but certainly he does not intend it in this account.

Himar (pl. *hamir* and *hammar*, masculine occupational noun). The etymology of this word is interesting for the translator. For it is proto-Semitic and pro-biotic in nature. The origin of the word can be found in Akkadian, Ugaritic, Aramaic, Urinic and indeed in the diuretic language groups. In essence, *Himar* captures that most stubborn of animals, the donkey. *Himar* can be used as a

------

pouring in a can of Pedigree Chum. I was astounded. "It's the best on the market," she howled apologetically, adding the mixer with the meat. "My father says that Pedigree Chum is the most balanced dog food on the market. If it's not to your liking, I promise you, Dr Rabie, I will also take you to Crufts. My father is a great breeder of dogs and has won many prizes there."

'I was astounded. Is this where our cultural misunderstandings lie? Mistranslations, poor little pretty student had taken my name completely out of context. Being a nubile materialist, she had put my name and ancestry down to evolution and so had assumed that I had undergone a thing evolutionists call "punctual equilibrium" that is - once my ancestors had stabilised as "donkeys", that is *jahsh*, they evolved into dogs. I was stupefied. We understood each other so well physically and her grades subsequently improved, but yet culturally and intellectually there was a chasm between us. And so, I decided to write this text and dedicate it to such students who wished to cross boundaries through cultural intercourse. I would like to think that I, in some small way, have managed to reduce all the conflicts and tension between the East and West with this brief text.'

synonym with *jahsh*, but the latter is more emphatic, unless the former is said in the Algerian dialect by a Berber from the Kabyle region. In such cases, it is advisable to run like the wind.

Haraam (adj.) - Forbidden or not permissible. The reader may have come across this word in the past, perhaps with a religious scholar who seems to use the word all the time. An obvious example is the case of pork; the flesh of swine is *haraam* - impermissible for Muslims. But one should note that sometimes, in the context of British fried chicken shops, you may encounter chicken wings, legs and breast injected with pork protein from the Netherlands and it can still be certified as *halal*.

Haraam then, has many different meanings. It can also mean inviolable. In old Ottoman homes, the quarter designated for the family was known as the *haraamlik*, the inviolable place where those who are not family cannot enter. Its opposite is *halal*, which the reader may come across again in the context of British fried chicken shops, but it has a far more profound meaning. *Ibn al-halal*, for instance, means 'son of a virtuous woman' or that he was born in the context of wedlock. *Ibn al-haraam* may mean the opposite. It is unclear what Ibn Fudayl intends when he mentions both.

Nemir (pl. *numur*), 'tiger'. The word is used synonymously with bravery, similar to the word *asad*.[6]

---

[6]   Note for the novice Arabic student just on the lower rungs of learning this most complex language: the pronunciation of *Asad* must be precise. I myself was directed by my Arabic teacher to Asda Supermarket fifty miles away from the university to learn this

Harb -The word 'war' is interestingly designated as feminine, instead of what one usually expects from such martial words in Arabic.[7]

Wahsh (pl. *wuhush*)- The words denote 'bestial wild fearlessness', without due regard for right and wrong. This theme is also found in Modern Standard Arabic and journalese, where one often reads the headlines 'Egypt First, Right or Wrong' and so on. Whilst the word is not used, it is this that is intended.

Subbar refers to 'prickly pears', the red and green fruit that grows at the tip of cactuses.

Bandora and *Tamatim* - these are words of foreign extraction. Usually Arabic can generate its own words by reworking its triliteral roots. Thus, for instance, Ha-La-Ka which encapsulates the meaning for 'destruction', by adding the additional letters IST becomes ISTAH-LA-KA which means 'to consume' and if one adds the suffix '-iyya' to the word, it comes to denote 'consumerism'- the implication being one will consume oneself to destruction. But such things aside, there are a few foreign words one finds in Quranic Arabic. 'Ibreeq' is one such example. But *tamatim* comes from 'tomato', as the reader will easily identify, and *bandora* comes from the Italian 'pomodoro', but in meaning they are the same. The difference lies in the way the

---

lesson. There was much mirth in that gathering on the part of my Arabic teacher.

[7]   See Jermaine Nigel, *The End of Patriarchy: How Arab Lexicographers Implemented EU Equality Directives in the Middle Ages: A Post-Colonial Neo-Conservative Reading*, Tusk (2011).

English pronounce the word 'tomato' putting emphasis on the 'o' and the Americans say 'tomato' changing the 'o' into an 'a' so it sounds like 'tomata'.

Diwan - can mean an oriental sofa, it can also mean administrative department in government or a poetry anthology. Thus, if one so wished, one could refer to Shakespeare's poetry collection as a *diwan*. Usually the reader will understand from the context what the word means and sometimes he will have to ask for clarification. This author, whilst chasing his fifty second visa stamp in Damascus, came across a mustachioed walrus, administrating sitting on a *diwan*, reading his own panegyric *diwan* in his *diwan*. When he asked me whether I liked his *diwan*, I was forced to ask him if he meant his sofa, collection of poetry or whether he meant his administrative department. I believe he meant his collection of poetry and I was arrested for violating my visa restrictions and subsequently deported to Iraq, where I came across a similar situation. The administrator did not intend his collection of poetry, but his oriental sofa and so I was deported to the Kingdom of Saudi Arabia where I found myself in similar circumstances. I told that administrator that it was the administrative department and he replied that it was *haraam* for me to enter. Such things are common occurrences in the Middle East.

Part I

I remember, as a young man, the first time I attended the classes of Sheikh al-Halabi at the Azhar University. Hundreds of eager students were sitting hunched forward on the floor, ready to record each of the sheikh's words. With an expression of pure calmness, the sheikh sat on the raised chair above the heads of the audience, waiting for any late comers to arrive. I remember how, after praising and glorifying God and passing salutations on the prophet, he had cleared his throat and said in a deep voice:

'If something is going to change, it is because people are going to change themselves. The only way to change themselves is to know themselves. The only way to know themselves is to break free of all the things someone else has taught them and find out for themselves. I only hope you, the future heirs of the prophets, will do this with caution.'[8]

---

[8]   P.351, *Al-Hikma lil-Daalin*, Muhammad Ayyub Darwish, Cairo, (1923). See the excellent biographical note on Sheikh al-Halabi, the translator Darwish, has found the rest of the lecture from a contemporary student that attended the same lecture as Ibn Fudayl which continues, 'who ever knows the truth by men is lost in a maze of misguidance. Seek the truth and you shall find its people if indeed you are following the truth. Sit with those that take you to certainty and away from pride and brings you closer to sincerity. Follow those who give you contentment and peace.

These were the words I remembered. These were the words I
have lived by ever since. I have from that day onwards sought out
many different lands in order to know myself and in my humble
little way change things for the better.

After the evening prayer, I went home and was promptly
questioned about the lecture given by the sheikh. I recounted to
my father everything I had heard and seen. As a consequence I was
thrashed. I repeatedly questioned him for the philosophical basis
for the punishment meted out. But to all extents and purposes,
he could not deliver a satisfactory answer that warranted such a
good thrashing. I found that in my life many a man gave me a
thrashing and yet none could give me a satisfactory answer to me
receiving this punishment.

Go to those who remove arrogance and give you humbleness.
Sit with those that prevent you from making enemies.' However,
Dr Darwish's translation has been critiqued by Oliver Shact who
has shown, in his fantastic article 'Al-Halabi's Jurisprudence and
Development of Prussian Legal Theory', *Bulletin of School of
Oriental and African Studies* (*BSOAS*) (1934), that the extract
is an augmentation from a Yemeni manuscript attributed to
Ahmad al-Haddad al-Husseini which claims that the words are
in fact those of the sheikh and Christian mystic Abu Maryam
al-Tikriti (d.1239). However, controversy has raged as the debate
was opened up by Hans Wiener. In his recent article, 'Hegel, al-
Halabi, and Houris in clashes of thought in Abbasid Christo-
Judean legal theory', *BSOAS* (2001), he has severely critiqued
al-Hikma as a translation and for Darwish's inconsistencies and
suggested that Shact's hypothesis has not been taken into account.
Newly discovered primary sources (Dead Sea Scrolls) attribute
the augmentation to the Ottoman scholar of Greek descent
al-Yunani. al-Hikma is practically obsolete as a translation and
highly unreliable, nevertheless it still provides a good amount
of source material for the 13th century. A new translation is
rumoured to being prepared by D.S. Richards. [Trans.]

I cannot quite remember the lecture of the venerable old sheikh, for unlike the rest I was not scribbling his words down; I relied on my excellent memory. My eyes had fallen on his thick fingers that were counting his rosaries as he spoke. I remember how beautiful his wooden beads were and pondered whether they were made of olive or sandalwood. Then I reflected on the chair he had been sitting on and the various coloured turbans that came in. I counted sixty green turbans, a hundred white ones, fifty-five black turbans, one yellow, two red and the others of non-descript colour were one hundred and twenty-one. It was a feat in arithmetic, I tell you. I deduced that the people of Egypt loved the white turban.

It is strange then how the son of a potter should now, after twenty years, find himself writing this book on the excellent and illustrious history of al-Homsi. Indeed, I have found out for myself what it means to be lost and then found. Had it not been for this great philosopher I would not be where I am today, at the pinnacle of wisdom and in the patronage of Sultan Mardanish.[9]

I feel that this level I have reached cannot be fully comprehended if I, by some means, do not preserve for posterity my meeting and the teachings that I gained from such an illustrious and magnificent man.

---

[9]   Governor Abdullah bin Mardanish (d.1165) was a native Spaniard, appointed by the Almoravid governor to rule Valencia. Ibn Mardanish began as a local potentate of Murcia who carved out a principality for himself. With the arrival of the Almohad power, he was appointed the governor of his principality. On appointment, he immediately moved to making Valencia the capital. See *Abdullah bin Mardanish, Exemplar Oriental Despot*, Gieves el-Rey, Santiago (1980).

George R. Sole

A NOTE ON THE PROVINCE OF VALENCIA AND ITS PEOPLES

I had come to Andalusia on the pretext that in the West, at least, wisdom and learning could be found. What I discovered was a complex and vibrant culture. The principality which I headed towards was that of Sultan Abdullah bin Mardanish, or as it is known, the province of Valencia. This province constitutes namely of two major cities. Valencia, a city famous for its rich yield in rice, citrus fruits, dates and commerce with the barbarians in the East and the Frankish seafaring statelets of the Western Roman Empire. These barbarians have brought over many commodities; namely slaves, durum wheat, fur and buffalo cheese. Although the trade has been unfruitful, the sultan has deemed trade with these barbarian nations an effective way of civilising these men of the sea that begin their perilous journey close to the island of Sicily. Despite its uncouth visitors, the city is splendid and magnificent with its gardens, white houses, winding alleyways and majestic mosques.

The second principal city is Murcia, founded by the Fatimids. It is a city famous for its scholars, mystics, learning and hardy fighting seamen. Its streets are dotted with every kind of school you can imagine, teaching jurisprudence, philosophy, mathematics, linguistics and even alchemy. Though poor in agricultural produce, it is famous for its excellent silk and cotton industry, handicrafts, leather and metalwork, not to mention its magnificent fishing fleets that bring in its silvery catch of tuna and sardines daily. The people deal mostly with the civilised world and tend to trade with Africa, China, India and of course Arabia.

The province itself is extremely rich, well-watered, irrigated, dotted with charming water wheels that bring forth a rich rice yield so healthy that Valencians have a festival to celebrate it. The yield is attributed to the phosphate rich Valencian manure that is unique in its texture, viscosity and scent (I have since learnt that it is considered a delicacy amongst certain Frankish tribes in the peninsula off the island of Sicily).[10] As a result, the land is capable of producing herbs, saffron, cumin, henna for the dyeing process and also various fruits like cherries, apples, pomegranates, figs, dates, grapes and almonds and even the occasional olive, which they export to the Frankish states who do not mind eating low quality foods. Apart from the breeding of goats, various bovine species and apiculture, the land also lends itself well to breed the famous Andalusian mule that wreaks havoc amongst the ranks of the Christian forces that occasionally threaten it. As for the natural wealth of the province, it manages to exploit its pines for charcoal and basket weaving, whilst the industrious population hew deep into the mountains to extract copper and iron ore. The abundance of marble and gold enables even the middling classes to embellish their villas with the white stone and their women with jewellery.

The geography lends itself to a great many fortresses to be built. With the arrival of the Almoravid power from North Africa and the growing tension with the Christian forces in the north, it has meant that the landscape has been dotted increasingly with fortresses and watch towers, making sure that there is complete safety in the land.

---

[10]   For an in-depth study of Frankish eating habits and culture, see the excellent *Frankish Culture in Southern Italy*, Valentina Viene, Neptune, (1989).

The character of the people in the province differs greatly. The majority of the populace are Muslims; they are either Arabized, pure Arab or of hardy Berber stock. You will find the Arabized population in the countryside and the city. Their temperament shows great intelligence, friendliness and generosity, but perhaps a tendency towards laziness. The pure Arabs, however, are confined to the cities or the land surrounding it. They are highly educated, civilised and display a zealousness towards their faith. Of the Berbers, you will find that most of them are from the tribe of Sanhaja. They confine themselves to the mountain regions and are distinct for being a hardy, crafty race, quick to temper and always veiling themselves in light blue shawls.

There are a significant number of Jews in the province of Valencia, who congregate mainly in the city. They are a highly intelligent people producing many a physician, trader, merchant, financier and scholar. Their temperament is reserved and you will find them to be extremely sensitive and cautious in their behaviour.

As for the Christians, there are very few of them in the province of Valencia; preferring to stay with their brethren in the north of the peninsula, apart from the odd hermit, they keep to themselves in the countryside. They are more often than not generous and kind people with a tendency towards superstition.

A NOTE OF THE POLITICS OF VALENCIA

In the *History of al-Andalus*, al-Kindi has related that, since the arrival of Islam, the peninsula enjoyed relative security with the Umayyad caliphs being firmly in control, the Christian kingdoms confined to the north of the peninsula. However, with its dissipation, Andalusia broke up into several principalities who fought each other for total supremacy. None were strong enough in achieving their aims. These rivalries were a disaster for Andalusia for these petty kings reached out towards the Christian kingdoms for protection. The Christian kingdoms, for a large tribute, would lay each of the petty kingdoms to waste, making Andalusia terribly weak. With the arrival of the Almoravids, a tenacious unity was achieved and the Christian kingdoms were pushed back.

The arrival of the Almoravid power in the peninsula caused the Christian kingdoms to become disconcerted. The Christian kings had been enjoying the full fruits of protecting the various principalities prior to their arrival (including the lands of Sultan Mardanish). King Alfonso of Leon Castile, for instance, arranged with the brave sultan that he, the king, would not raid and massacre the population of Valencia in return for a considerable sum every year. The king, however, promised that he would raid and massacre the principality of Seville for an extra fee. The brave sultan duly paid it by means of taxes on the export of Valencian manure abroad.[11] The arrangement was a fruitful one and Alfonso's kingdom became prosperous. Alfonso even became a patron of the Arts at the University of Valencia for giving the sultan such excellent advice. The king's newly

---

[11]   P398, *Valencian Manure, Globalisation and the Shaping of Western Europe*, Caterina Pinto, Napoli, (1988). There is considerable evidence to suggest that there were riots all over Spain when this tariff was introduced. Dr Pinto argues it depressed the European markets and development for a century. Not only did it see a decline in the dietary health of the population of Western Europe, but it also made Europe turn towards the Atlantic to rid itself from its dependency on Valencian manure. In her insightful study, she suggests that even the venture of Columbus was not really a search for India, rather, Columbus was looking for that mythical South American phosphate-rich manure called Guano.

found wealth meant that he could afford to have litanies sung
for the great men in all his churches. However, the arrival of the
Almoravids in Andalusia turned off this supply of gold like a tap.

The Almoravids took the war to their borders and regained
the lost territories. The Christian king was understandably
upset for he worried, it is said, that the churches would sing
no litanies for the forgiveness of his sins. The king consulted
his notables and two suggestions were made. One, that they
should ride across the lands of Andalusia, raid, pillage and
ravage the land (as was the custom). But this he felt was too
unoriginal, for his cousin, King Alfonso el-Battlador of Aragon,
had ingeniously raided deep into Andalusian territory and, as a
display of his might, had bathed in the Mediterranean! The King
of Leon Castile felt that he must do something different. His
Archbishop, a pious austere man, suggested that he pay gold for
a magnificent church where they would pray for the destruction
of the Almoravids. The pious king found that a costly option
and wrote to the University of Valencia, who wrote back saying
he should write a letter to the Pope, their caliph, to gather an
army from all over Western Christendom, and to collect a tithe
from the barbarian peasants in order to repel the Almoravids
from the peninsula. Thus, a great military expedition was born.
But the Almoravids managed to remain in power and so too did
Sultan Abdullah bin Mardanish.

THE EXCELLENT AND ILLUSTRIOUS
HISTORY OF AL-HOMSI

Now begins the biography and the auspicious meeting with the
wise and great philosopher al-Homsi. But before I embark on

this narration, it is important to relate the background that lead me to this great man.

Having journeyed and looked into the peculiar nature of these peoples of the Iberian Peninsula, I found myself confined mostly to two areas in the province of Sultan Mardanish, namely Murcia and Siyasa.[12] I was in Murcia for its excellent scholasticism. I avoided many of the lectures given by the city's notable and famous scholars. I did not wish to constrain my mind to Quranic exegesis, purification of the soul, logic, rhetoric, metaphysics, mathematics, science, botany, linguistics or explanations on Imam Malik's *Muwatta*.[13] Rather, I wanted to free my mind, thus every night I attended invigorating lectures ranging from the chemical excellencies of Valencian manure, held in a farm of sorts outside the city gates, to the merits of the Maliki legal school over the Hanafites given by young gifted eighteen year olds. I also attended numerous debates on the primordial essence of being and the Platonist conception of the perfect camel delivered by the eminent scholar al-Himyari. My mind was refreshed and danced with the wonders that I saw and learnt there. But what drew me away to the town of Siyasa was when I attended a lecture given by one of the students that hailed from there, entitled 'The Existence of the Non-Existent'. I marvelled at the young man's logic, his eloquence, his flawlessness in grammar, his rhetoric and felt that if such men can be produced in such a small village, then I too must visit that place. For, after all, was I not in search of enlightenment?

---

[12] See the in-depth study, *Siyasa: A Study in Freedom*, Bernford Lewes, Paramount (2007).

[13] Imam Malik was the founder of the Maliki school.

After all, had I not crossed the seven seas, spent aeons all over the world just to find exactly that? I decided that very day that I would harness my donkey, load my books and notes, and ride out in search of this curious little town.

When I arrived, I found the place to be, to say the least, exotic. Siyasa, according to the historians of our day, descends from Berber stock, the *kilab* tribe, to be exact; they are considered fiercely tribal. These people, it is said, were so clannish and jealous of their lineage that they only married within their tribe or immediate family. Generations of coupling has meant that it is very difficult to tell Siyasans apart; you could even forgive yourself for thinking each a brother, sister, mother and father. Their eyes are very large, their heads unusually small, their frames robust. Every Siyasan is somehow related to each other and often a Siyasan mother will find that it is not her son that is eating at the table, but her grandfather's brother's sister's cousin. The spectacle is rather amusing and one often holds one's belly and chortles at the drama! Siyasans never insult another Siyasan's brother, sister, mother or father for fear he might unknowingly be insulting his own. Such insults may result in death and, if said by an outsider, war. Siyasans are prone to war due to their physical toughness. As a result, they boast to all those who will hear them that they display the finest qualities in man: intellect and bellicosity.

After betaking myself some lodgings, a small cozy room in a travellers' inn in the heart of the city, I immediately sought news of the two great scholars of the small provincial town. These two renowned sons of Siyasa were Sheikh Majd ed-Deen and Sheikh Nur ed-Deen. They were the two main legal authorities in the city.[14] It is worth for a moment to know just a bit about their deeds, sayings and their achievements before I recount the tale.

It is said that from a very young age these two boys were unlike their peers in intellect, logic and inquisitiveness. They had none of the slow movements or slurred speech that young Siyasans seemed to display. Rather their handwriting, their ability to deal with morphology, and rules of grammar was celebrated by the city as a whole. None of the typical characteristics of Siyasans were found. So sharp and quick witted were they that some amongst the Siyasans whispered maliciously, that their mothers may have played false. The Murcian teachers that lived in the city were astounded, amazed. Could it be that Siyasa would stop importing their scholars from Murcia and perhaps produce some of their own?! They were amazed at how these two sons argued with them over irrelevancies. Sometimes when the time for afternoon prayer would approach, the two young men would argue with each other of the exact position of where the hands should be placed when in the standing position. Both, it seemed, held diametrically opposite positions; it meant of course, that they could never be the best of friends. Nevertheless, both realised that they were mutually dependent on each other, not only because they were somehow brothers, but also uncles and each other's grandfather.

The two, however, displayed one deficiency: their poor physical condition. But it did exempt them from the arduous

---

[14]   See *Ibn Khallikan's Biographical Dictionary*, Lane, (1889), for further biographical information. See also *Oriental Scholasticism, Market Economics: A Marxist Approach*, M. Amis, Columbia, (2002), and *Al-'Alama al-Andalusi fii 'Asr Muluk at-Tawa'if*, Abdullah Majdi, Cairo, (1967).

military service that every Siyasan male was legally bound to render the state. The Murcian scholars also felt that it would be beneficial if they could be sent far far away from Siyasa, in order to study with the masters of jurisprudence, tradition, theology and so forth. They petitioned the governor for a generous stipend and received it. With this generous stipend, the two young men were forced to travel together to Damascus. The journey through North Africa on to Cairo was indeed a fruitful one. The two intellectuals discussed and argued over many topics, for example, on the exact number of angels in heaven, the precise position of the throne of God, the exact time of Judgment Day and many other interesting topics. One can only imagine how these two fellows must have ridden their donkeys discussing, flaying their arms up, throwing the odd prod at each other with their stick. The sight must have been marvellous!

The arguing reached new levels in Cairo. Sheikh Majd ed-Deen received a bruise on his right eye, and Sheikh Nur ed-Deen received a broken nose. The argument was about the best route to take to Damascus. After much wrangling, they reached a compromise, and decided to take a much longer route to the port of Aqaba and cross the Red Sea. However, the Lord, Great and Glorious is He, decreed that the fishing vessel they had commandeered be swept to a small fishing village known as Jeddah. Here they were accosted by Feisal, a Bedouin chief who, impressed by the number of books that they carried, took the two young men away deep into the deserts of Arabia. There he introduced them to his simple young brother Abd el-Aziz, who was also impressed by the

number of books they possessed.[15] The two young students
lived with these simple Bedouins for exactly two weeks. The
brothers then decided that it would be better for the unity of
the tribe if they be split apart. So each brother took one of
the students and parted from each other. Over the ten years
that passed, the two students devised their own complete
and unique principles of Jurisprudence. In the process of this
fruitful intellectual exchange, the two patrons, namely Feisal
and Abd el-Aziz, declared Holy War on each other and robbed

---

[15] For an introduction on the Bedouin please read *The Bedouin:
      An Anthropological Study*, Jay Witherspoon Larkin, Chattilion,
      (1999); the book is remarkable, as Larkin spent several months
      with the Bedouins in Damascus and Aleppo, Baghdad, Dubai, and
      Jeddah. He cuts a starkly different picture of the Bedouin. Using
      newspapers, dictionaries, colouring-in books, modern literature
      and film he contrasts the Arab with the Bedouin and finds that
      they are essentially the same cunning species. He discovers that
      they are suited for the desert and still possess that aggressive nature
      that allows them to have an amazing propensity for violence. He
      shows, using deep analysis of his dictionaries and their minds,
      that the Bedouin has an inherent need to subdue nature. But his
      impotence in subduing nature means that he is forced to take on a
      religion of submission which leads to an inherent need to subdue
      his women. Larkin theorizes that, as a result, the Bedouin, confines
      his women to the house and/or dresses them up in various alluring
      garbs. The conclusion is that within the modern Arab mind
      remains the untamed Bedouin that wants out and seeks to destroy
      civilisation itself in order to achieve its dastardly aims. He proposes
      that if this Bedouin mentality is understood and catered for, many
      political solutions can be reached. The study is a breakthrough in
      the Arab-Israeli conflict, according to Professor Levy Strauss. The
      study is of course extremely controversial and has been criticised
      by Dr Vitty Volgare (and other Israeli scholars), in her famous
      article 'Foucault, Kafka, The Da Vinci Code, Arab Masculinity and
      Female Bisexuality: A Deconstructionist Reading', *Journal for Arab
      Understanding* (JFAU), Haifa, (2003).

each other's goat and camel herds. God, Great and Wise is He, decreed that after ten years the two students, now sheikhs in their own right, could buy their freedom and return to Siyasa. Upon their return, they taught the populace all that they knew. It was, quite literally, the beginning of a new era in the history of this quaint town. The inhabitants petitioned the Sultan of Valencia to invest the two sheikhs with legal authority. And so they became the first native jurists that Siyasa had ever brought forth.

When I arrived, however, a healthy and vigorous debate was ranging all over Siyasa. The debate, as far as I know, had lasted for up to three years and was coming to its conclusion with the arrival of the auspicious al-Homsi. Fortune, however, would have it that I, Ibn Fudayl, should be one of the keys to this great debate, for I too am not a bad jurist, lest one forget.

Now I shall proceed to give you the peculiarities of this intellectual debate which refreshes the soul so. Several years ago, a merchant by the name of Yusuf, from the beautiful city of Mosul, had come to trade in Murcia. He was like many of his people, difficult to comprehend. A silk merchant by trade, he had come to Murcia for that specific purpose. His temperament was austere and therefore did not like to take up his residence in Murcia, neither did he like to take up residence in the grandiose villas surrounding the city. Instead, the pious man took up lodging in a simple white washed house in Siyasa. He liked Siyasa for its all-pervading scent of jasmine and sheer simplicity. The city was resplendent with date palms, olive, orange and pomegranate trees. The people too were helpful but he had to speak slowly and at times use gestures for them to comprehend his accent.

The town was so simply designed that it was nearly impossible for him and the inhabitants to get lost. And yet the governor, out of consideration no doubt, had placed visible maps telling the visitor exactly where he was in the town. The town itself was divided into four quarters, with a main road going from south to north and a main road crossing it from east to west. Where the roads crossed, the governor had put up a building of sorts. It was placed there, following Roman tradition, which required that there be a 'grand perspective' for the inhabitants to take in their city in all its glory. The design of the building was rather ingenious. When I saw it I was forced, forced I tell you, to bring out the finest paper I had bought from a crafty Chinese fellow in Samarqand and draw it in order for future generations to see. It was to all appearances made of pine wood (I made sure it was by knocking on it). It possessed a door whereby the ever-watchful sentinel stood watch in all his martial finery. Just below this wooden building were four large wheels which moved if one harnessed it to some horses. I and the sentinel used to sit inside for hours sipping fortifying Chinese green tea, just admiring the interior of the building.[16] To return, the second function the building served was for its distinction and prominence, so in case any of the inhabitants got lost, he could always navigate himself to his home from there. The governor had placed the sentinel there in order to direct lost souls back to their homes. Each quarter had its name written in bold and had been assigned a mosque.

I am told that Yusuf liked after a hard day's trading, to retire to his lodgings in the north-eastern quarter and attend the

---

[16]   P567, *The Evolution of the Horse Cart and American Frontier Expansion*, Robert McDermot, Teshcen, (1978).

evening prayer at the North-East Mosque (it is also known as
'mosque number two' by the locals). Yusuf was a sensitive soul;
as his stay in Siyasa became prolonged, he became increasingly
disconcerted. His trade began to suffer, he could not deal with
the business-like Murcians properly, for the whispers in the
mosque and the town began to bear down on his mind and he
would often lose sleep over it. Until eventually, after a bad day of
trade, he could take it no more and decided to remove the cloud
of doubt that had settled on his brow.

Yusuf's predicament was not an easy one, for I myself, known
as I am for my strength in mental character, have been afflicted by
doubts and crisis in faith.[17] So much so that at one point, I could

---

[17] Other great scholars have written on similar spiritual crises; see the
famous autobiography of al-Ghazzali the Sufi mystic and theologian,
Al-Munkidh min ad-Dalala, Abu Hamid al-Ghazzali, Beirut, (1987).
Even more relevant could be the spiritual crisis experienced by
artists in Europe such as Rembrandt. See *Growth of Rembrandt's
Spiritual Crisis*, R. Fuller, Phoenix, (1976), as Fuller makes a detailed
analysis of the great Dutch artist's life and points out that Rembrandt
struggled throughout his life with the problem of the beard.
Whether he should keep it long or short was a question that afflicted
his career and is expressed in his art; for example, his painting of
Samson and Delilah (1636) shows clearly his Freudian struggle
and leaves the audience asking themselves: should he have a short
or long beard? For ultimately, this is a question that plagues most
men and sometimes women. His personal struggle is manifested
in his self-portraits, compare the self-portrait in 1628, where he
initiates the long beard, and the self-portrait, 1668-69, where he is
free of the beard; a complete volte-face. The art-critic Fuller quite
rightly points out that his artistic crisis in his paintings and his
subsequent falling into debt was direct result of public indignation
and his spiritual turmoil, regarding the state of his beard. Perhaps
the strongest indication that he was deeply influenced by the Siyasan
ideologues is shown in 1626, when he depicts Anna, accused by
Tobit of stealing a kid goat; the implication is that she stole it to

do nothing but eat and sleep and be on my own. I could not deliver my lectures. In fact, I can well remember the embarrassment that I suffered in front of my students as I taught the significance of the Pythagorean secular circularism in relation to the Neolithic platonic square. My hypothesis of the possibilities that the hedonistic square circle's relation to ephemeral monotheistic polytheism held the key to the essence of being, namely earth, water, wind and fire, was simply not grasped. They could not understand that this Hellenistic conception of the humours had infused the whole world. I could not, for the life of me, elucidate this medicinal perspective of the universe, so that I was forced to endure humiliation. Even a buffoon, a water carrier to be precise, accused me of Semantics![18] Although I had the scoundrel thrown out, the embarrassment I suffered as I drew the triangle wrong, brought out a nervous fever inside so that my hands were shaking and all I could do was utter the word 'whimsical' for three days in a row. Now, I realise it was God's way of showing me the arrogance that I had displayed. That all my efforts had been for nothing, that I had not been sincere, that I had craved only the fame, position and wealth. It was only after I freed myself, leaving my teaching position, my slave girl, my three month old child, my home for the open road that I recovered. Faith was restored immediately, as if a Gabriel had lowered his wings on

---

shave it. Rembrandt unfortunately never resolved his personal and artistic crisis and died as a result of it. See also *Jihad al-Fannan al-'Azeem li-Rembrandt,* Francois Boutfliqa Arkon, Beit Jabri, (1989).

[18]   For a clear introduction to the intricate complexities of what is, in essence, the foundational basis of Evolutionary Darwinism read 'Dostoyevsky's Gnosticism: Explaining the Square Circle, a Marxist Theism under the Lens of the Gramscian Agnostics Challenge', Arthur Probotsky, *Philosophy Quarterly,* (1989).

me, after five miles of strenuous, thirsty and hungry walking, I reached my answer and turned home. Very soon I delivered my most famous and adulated lecture talked about by the city of Damascus to this very day. My lecture on 'Plotinus's hermeneutic linguistic temporalism' has given birth to a whole new school.[19] So one must excuse him, for every man, even great men, are sometimes forced to tread this road of Doubt.

---

[19] P99, *A Comparison of the Moghul Invasions, and the Great Damascene Riots of the Ayyubid Age: Numbers and Casualty: A Statistical Survey*, P. M. Hult, Everywoman, (1980). Professor Hult believes that though the casualties were more or less the same with the Moghul invasion beating the Damascene riot in deaths (but not in casualties and injuries), the Damascene riots could have been more detrimental for the region. It set back the region in terms of progress by about a hundred years. In fact, some like Dr Donna Prodi, in her brilliant post-feminist deconstructionist reading, *Viva l'Europa, Viva l' Occidente*, Donna Prodi, Il Calamaio, (1999), asserts that the Damascene bloodbath was the key to European growth, for the depopulation of Oriental intellectuals and their emigration to Europe, particularly to the merchant states of Italy, meant that their expertise of state craft were utilised to develop the foundation of a democratic process and, in the case of Italy, unification. Their scientific expertise and ability to translate Arabic texts into Latin meant that information flowed freely into the Occident. The birth of Protestantism, in particular Calvinism, combined with the Colombus's opening up of America and Europe's independence from Valencian manure meant that this fledgling unity and progress could be achieved. She concludes controversially that had the Damascene blood bath not occurred, modern Europe and indeed the West would not have come about and left the Orient to linger in its oriental sensuality and languor that prevented industrialisation. Dr Caterina Pinto gave a recent paper at the Orientale, entitled: 'Stabbio di Valencia'. She has rubbished this theory and outlined that only the independence from Valencian farming products allowed for industrialisation. South American Guano allowed Europe to feed its population and only once it could feed its population, could it progress to its freedom.

For a time, Yusuf had prayed at mosque number two, along with his brothers in faith. He could not understand the murmurs that his fellow worshippers uttered when they saw him at the mosque. He did not want to believe that Siyasans were an unkind and ungenerous people. It was as if he were doing something wrong and yet did not know the reason. The caprices of Fate, however, decreed that he should be sent a herald. As he prayed sincerely one evening, a young fellow, who could barely sport his own beard, advised him that there was simply no evidence or authority for him to keep such a short beard. His lips quivered, his body trembled. So it was true! He turned his head and scoured the mosque and realised that everyone had the same length that Sheikh Majd ed-Deen himself wore. Even, it seemed, the young pubescent boy who addressed him had put one on in order to follow the example of the sheikh! Yusuf, full of zeal, bought the best olive oil, sunned his beard, fertilised it with finest coconut oil from India and followed the exercises that were prescribed by the young fellow; which, I am told, allowed the blood in his veins to reach the desired parts of his face. After a week of vigorous growing, he reached an acceptable length. When he arrived at mosque number two, he was received by the congregation like he was a long-lost brother returned home. And though there were some pedants who harboured some suspicion and rancour, inspecting closely his facial growth with their wooden rulers just to get the exact measurements, he was accepted amongst most of the band of brothers with laughter and joy.

However Great and Glorious is He! He decided that Yusuf should find himself being led by one particularly quiet member of the congregation to pray the evening prayer at the

South-Western Mosque (mosque number four). There he found
that the men all possessed beards that were shorter. At one point,
our dear fellow feared for his life. He was amongst a band of
savages who threatened to cut open his neck with their very gazes.
However, the illustrious Sheikh Nur ed-Deen seeing that the poor
fellow was a lost soul, intervened. He elucidated with great verve
and clarity the fallacy of keeping such a long beard. Yusuf was so
convinced by his arguments that, in front of everyone in mosque
number four, he cut off his magnificent long beard that very
evening. Adulation filled the crowd of mosque number four; men
recited a Siyasan version of panegyric poetry in his honour.[20] But
those hypnotic lines of verse soon faded, as he left that night, the
shadows of doubt crept in over his one eyebrow.

It was related to me, on the authority of Abdullah bin Khaldun
on the authority of Ahmad bin Shams on the authority of Abdu
bin Sadr ed-Deen or Abu Layth, the sentinel of Siyasa, that the
next day he stepped in to mosque number two for answers. The
mosque was not embellished with delicate calligraphy, nor was its
shelves filled with volumes of books, commentaries and several
centuries of scholarship like the mosques of Mosul; rather it was
harshly austere. Yusuf met the Imam Sheikh Majd ed-Deen. He
found Sheikh Majd ed-Deen to be a very sombre man with an
extraordinary long beard that reached down to his stomach.

---

[20] P236, *Arabic Panegyric Poetry*, Nabil Alam, Beirut, (1978). According
to Dr Alam, traditional Arabic panegyric poetry was complex in
nature using complex word play and metaphors. Siyasan panegyric
poetry was far simpler in construction. It consisted namely of
one line or at the most two lines. The lines were recited over and
over, sometimes up to a hundred or two hundred times. The poet
or the reciters conveying various shades of meaning through the
intonation of their voice.

The Travels of Ibn Fudayl   21

He was also distinguished for possessing one tooth or rather fang that protruded out of his mouth. I have marvelled at this fang myself and I am amazed at how the grand sheikh consumes his food! Glory be to Him who creates men in all shapes and sizes! Further, he possessed a deep brown mark on his forehead due to his excessively long prostrations. The carpet that he prayed on five times a day was exceptionally rough. Abdullah bin Khaldun has told me personally that he has seen the sheikh leading the congregational prayer, where he remains in prostration, from the noon prayer to the afternoon prayer, in the very same prostrating position, wailing or quaking in front of his God so loudly that even mosque number four can hear it. Majd ed-Deen at first seemed disturbed by the shortness of Yusuf's beard and suspected him to be an assassin sent by the powers that be. But once Yusuf explained his predicament, the stern man softened. Yusuf pointed out that in Mosul and many other parts of the Islamic world, the length of the beard mattered little. The sheikh became gentle and interrupted Yusuf. He asserted, as if Yusuf were a little child, that the beard was in his own words: 'The very pillar of the faith, its length was as long as one's faith.'[21]

He decreed that those who considered the short beard as part of the faith were innovators, possibly apostates and had no philosophical footing to stand on. The one toothed man then proceeded to give him a private lesson that some say lasted for a week. Others say it lasted all of the holy month of Ramadan. The sincerity of Yusuf was clear, at great loss to his trade, he set about

---

[21]   For an in depth understanding of the beard and its philosophical underpinnings see *The Political Spectrum of the Beard and its History*, Gregor Mandel, Teshcen, (1998).

studying with the great man. Study, as he saw it, was worship.
Out of those gruelling days of study, debate, and worship he
was saved from his own ignorance. He had been illuminated,
he too wanted the mark of prayer on his forehead. Sheikh Majd
ed-Deen was pleased with his newly found disciple and showed
him the secrets of secrets; he showed him how to achieve the
brown prayer mark that would save one from the Fires of Hell.[22]

At the end of this search for knowledge, Yusuf felt that he had
a responsibility to proselytize what he had learnt. He had to save
his brothers in faith! He needed to spread the doctrine of the
Long Beard. He reasoned that God would ask him on the Day
when there is no shade about the knowledge he had been given.
What would he say? How could he turn up to his Lord in such a
state of abject misery? He packed in his business, even though he
had creditors waiting for him in Mosul and Baghdad, and decided
to tread on God's path. His brothers tried to dissuade him from
his path and thought him insane. He thought them infidels. I
am told he began his new life with gusto. He began by studying

---

[22]   In *Sirr min al-Asrar fi Obodiyaa Rabbi il-Alameen*, Majd ed-Deen
as-Siyaasi al-Andalusi, translated by Eduard du-Lavatoire, Cairo,
(1978), the sheikh instructs the novice to 'approach from 47-degree
acute angle the rough carpet, made of reed or palm fibre, in perfect
sincerity. Ask the Lord that one needs His mercy and blessing.
Keep on rubbing the rough carpet as you supplicate, until the skin
is removed and rough. Do not stop O brother, but continue until
your voice can be heard in the most distant corners of the city. Your
repentance must be painful and sincere. Keep the forehead rough
for a week and continue in sincere repentance, until the skin on the
forehead has become rough and tough like leather. So no pain can
be felt and through this way within the week God will grant you
the prayer mark that it takes some men of piety to achieve in one
hundred years of sincere prayer'.

a treatise that gave a point by point refutation of the short beard and memorized it within three days. He wrote an eloquent and moving treatise on 'The Necessity of the Long Beard' and spread it amongst the populace single handedly.[23] Eventually, his efforts resulted in the persuasion of the wise Sheikh Majd ed-Deen and himself to set up the party of the glorious long beards in the north-eastern quarter of Siyasa. They declared in their political manifesto that the elimination of the short beards was a moral necessity, even if it meant *extirpation*.[24]

---

[23] The untranslated manuscript can be found at the Bodleian Library, Oxford.

[24] This is hard to translate. In Arabic it is far more eloquent 'Hizb el-Lehyat at-Taweela al-Shareefa', [Trans.]. For a book on the party, see *The Party of the Siyasan Beards: The Origins of Western Democratic System and Revolution*, J. Hennessy, Longchamp, (2007). Professor Hennessy makes startling similarities between this period and the Western democratic system. He identifies that even the British constitution is not untainted by the Long and the Short beard controversy. To the great uproar of traditional historians such as E.J. Carr, Fritsch Fischer, and the French *Annales* School, he asserts with considerable evidence, that Disraeli was a Short Beard and Gladstone was a Long Beard. Gladstone was, in reality, ousted because he was impotent in growing one. Professor Hennessy hypothesizes that the political spectrum has been under constant flux. As a result, the Short Beard and the Long Beard i.e. Masonic influences of these two Oriental forces have radically altered the political landscape of New Labour Britain. The country seems to swing from Short Beardism to Long Beardism, as we enter the new millennium, Short Beardism seems to be ascendant, as one notices in the attack on the Long Bearded population of Europe. However, in the Orient Long Beardism is alive and a growing threat. Thus, the professor contends with great authority that the sporadic long beard uprisings in Afghanistan, Iraq and other countries is all an expression of a movement to assert the truth of the Long Beards. Some of Professor Hennessy's theories are, admittedly, far-fetched.

God, great and glorious is He, decreed that on the same hour
as the two men declared their manifesto to the world. In the
South-Western Mosque, the great Sheikh Nur ed-Deen stood up,
waved his staff like a sword and uttered a rousing spellbinding
sermon; the meaning of which, if understood, could move
even the armies of the most savage Germanic tribes beyond
al-Andalus! The simple words of Siyasan eloquence rang out
in the four corners of the mosque. 'Brethren!' he screamed, his
face red and fiery, 'in order for us to establish the short beard
in our family it is important for us to start at the top.[25] We must
follow the correct methodology and spread the correct message
amongst the people, we must have an overhaul of government
and use any means at our disposal. We are currently in talks
with local notables who fully agree that our cause *is* just. Can
you not see it, men, that if we lose today, even the great caliph
of Baghdad will sport a long beard? That shall be the end of us
and the extinction of Truth and Justice.[26] We stand for Truth, the
establishment of the short beard is incumbent on every Muslim,

There is no evidence whatsoever that Balfour, Randolph and Winston
Churchill were closet Long Beards. However, he has considerable
evidence to support the view that Lord Salisbury was the Masonic
Grandmaster of the Secret Long Beard Party in Britain. Across
the Atlantic, Franklin Roosevelt, was his opposite counterpart.
Some other significant events in history are more plausible: the
imprisonment of Nelson Mandela, the Apollo landings, the loss of
Jose Mourinho for Chelsea FC, the assassination of Che Guevara,
JFK, Malcolm X and John Lennon, Thatcher (a prominent Long
Beardista) all are meticulously documented and proven.

[25] *Origins of the Marxist Leninism*, Igor Abrahamovich, Pravda, issue
34567, October 15, (1923).

[26] See for an introduction to the short beard justice system *Theory
of Short Beard Justice,* Justin Rawls, Atticus, (1987): he draws a
remarkable parallel between the Siyasan political conflict and the

young, male, female, old, weak, disabled, it does not matter what you are: if you possess a beard you keep it short.[27] We must remove these ancient polytheistic practices brought in from the fire worshippers of Persia.[28] This, friends, is Siyasa. This, my friends, is a land of the short beard!'[29]

This is just a mere extract that I gathered. However, afterwards, I also gleaned from the vast library of the University of Valencia that the speech was far more extensive. Apparently, according to the archives, he is said to have given a flawless analysis of the situation. He concluded that the only reason that the Christian King of Leon Castile was so successful was because none of the believers that repelled him sported a single short beard. Not a single short beard! It was in his own words 'outrageous'. This was the reason the war was being lost and Andalusia was slowly vanishing, until one day it would merely be a whisper to the Believers and a posterior of the Christian kingdoms. Every day he proselytized on his raised pulpit saying the word 'outrageous', according to some estimations, 540 times. He urged his followers, until his beard was wet with tears, that there was an impellent need to return to its pristine unblemished values. Following a week of lectures on the subject, on Friday the exhausted gaunt sheikh ascended his pulpit and declared, in no unclear terms to the massive crowd that gathered, that there must be a new order.

---

landmark case in Regina Versus Edward S. Beard, the monumental case that brought Asquith's liberal party down and split it irrevocably.

[27] P238, *The Party of the Siyasan Beards: The Origins of Western Democratic System and Revolution*, J. Hennessy, Longchamp, 2007.

[28] P563, Hennessy.

[29] P890, Ibid.

'Either,' he shook his fist and banged his feet on his pulpit, 'you are with us or you are against us!'[30]

He shook his fist so hard that day that some of his believers say a clot formed in his brain and it lead to his eventual martyrdom.

Indeed, the grand sheikh could never be accused of hypocrisy. It is related to me by a trusty source from whom I purchased some excellent goat cheese, that Sheikh Nur ed-Deen applied the law to the letter. A few weeks after his amazing lectures he, as was his custom on Friday afternoon, took a walk in the picturesque and undulating fields just outside the provincial town. There he beheld a goat that had an exceptionally long beard. He, a man of principle, immediately set off in pursuit and displayed amazing athleticism for such a rotund old scholar, leaping and bounding after the goat until he caught up with the four-legged beast and wrestled it down, he brought out his scissors (for all short beards carry one) and measuring implements, and ritually trimmed the beard to its desired length.[31] The people, namely the farmers who watched the events were so affected that they immediately converted to Short Beardism. With the zeal of the converted, they left their ripe harvest and set about trimming their goats in the same fashion. Soon, within a few days, the whole surrounding countryside was in tumult. Most had converted their goats to Short Beardism except for a few, who either out of stubbornness or faith remained true to the Order of the Long Beard.[32] Lo! Some

[30] P1038, *Ibid*. According to modern estimates, the numbers that attended his seminars range from a scale of 5 to 500 people.

[31] See 'Origins of Masonic Symbolism and Ritual', Jay H. Berluscone, *BSOAS*, 1945, and in particular the case of Jack the Ripper.

[32] An order founded by Sheikh Majd ed-Deen that promised to further the philosophical cause of the Long Beard. It was similar to

fellows in their zeal began to kidnap even the long bearded goats and relieved them of their beards and some, God have mercy, were even mutilated!

However, I hear some men say: should one fault men for their zeal? But still, the intellect questions, at times, the extent of one's zeal. I mean, I consider myself to be a man of zeal and activity. After all, have I not crossed the lands of China, Hindustan, Persia to arrive at such an outpost that stabs out at the Atlantic? And yet were I a proponent of this ideology would I, Ibn Fudayl, do the same? Indeed, Man can be put into various moral mazes that have no exit. Will I not feel for the sorry state of our four legged friends?[33] Sometimes, when my soul feels heavy by this dilemma, I retrace those very footsteps to walk amongst those fields of history to ease the soul. And to this very day, when I spy a lonesome goat far far from home, I cannot for the life of me help but burst out in tears. Last time I visited, I heard the 'ba' of a lonely goat, followed by a second more melancholic 'baa'. I felt her loss, my strangeness, my alienation in this ephemeral and yet so Pythagorean prison, so temporally eternal that I impulsively embraced her as if it were my sister. Together we shared each other's loneliness; I offered my companion some medicinal

the *ikhwan as–Safa,* the brethren of purity, a group of philosophers that had been formed in the 11th century. The group was known for writing the fifty-one epistles that professed free thinking and a search for an all embracing truth. By the 12th century they were already wide spread in Andalusia. See *Islamic Theology and Oriental Hedonism*, Patricia Crowe, Abacus, (2007).

[33] See *Do Androids Dream of Electric Sheep?*, Philip K. Dick, Viagra, (1978), analyses in depth Ibn Fudayl's philosophical position. See also 'The Roots of al-Gore's Oriental Environmentalism', David Brooks, *BSOAS*, (2007).

fermented grape juice, that I use every day to treat my fits of migraines, and she drank it straight from the bottle. Likewise, the goat, sensing my empathy, made me a turn by offering me its milk. It stretched out its only erect teat for me to drink from. Its wholesome thick salty white milk was so rich and wholesome that I could not help to take another draught. So different was it from its usual milk one finds in Valencia.

To return from my own predicament, of course, any political observer will tell you that it caused absolute uproar in the town of Siyasa. For it went against a decree that the Long Beard party had pushed in the Siyasan council that everyone in the town and its surrounding areas must adopt the Long Beard.[34] These atrocities against these grazing innocents was intolerable! The one toothed sheikh could stand it no more, he organised parties that did double night patrols in order to protect those goats that already remained on his path. Many

---

[34]   P456, 'On the Free Will of Goats', H. Malik, *BSOAS*, (2003). This is not factually correct, according to al-Kindi's *Tarikh al-Andalus*, there were extensive debate between Sheikh Majd ed-Deen and Yusuf al-Mawsuli about whether to include animals and livestock in the decree. Here Yusuf's bold zeal pushed the soft gentle manners of Sheikh Majd ed-Deen to submit to the inclusion of goats. However, major disagreement fell on the cockcrow or rooster: did it have a beard? In other words, did it possess a soul? A whole philosophical debate ensued: Yusuf believed it was and provided hundred and fifteen proofs which the sheikh in sheer exercise of political will refuted point by point. He gave his own reasons for why it was not a beard. The private debate lasted for ten days. The alliance could not be broken, but Yusuf conceded to Sheikh Majd ed-Deen's request not to include roosters as being covered under the manifesto. See also chapter 9 of the great beard expert, 'The Significance of the Rooster in Oriental Thought', *The Political Spectrum of the Beard and its History*, Gregor Mandel, Teshcen, (1998).

a night would he lose tears just thinking about such crimes. The venerable scholar developed such a keen ear that he could hear, just by the tremble of the goat's vocal cords, that it was oppressed. He knew, by staring into the dumb eyes of the animal, he knew by the taste of the cud whether it had suffered abomination. He was so effected, that sometimes, in full view of the people, he would sit kneeling on the surrounding hills, arms raised in sincere prayer, his silhouette beseeching God that He not punish his beloved homeland and commit it to the fate of Sodom and Gomorrah.

'Lord!' he would shout at the top of his voice, 'O Lord, save us from this terrorism! I beseech you! Deliver us!'

All night until dawn he would remain wailing. Wailing even for the short bearded goats and pointing his crooked accusing finger at them for choosing such an abhorrent position.[35] Then sadness would enter his heart that perhaps even they would find themselves in Hell because of other men's actions.

His party could bear it no more; there was to be a clash of wills. This inevitable clash of wills was aggravated and brought closer to its conclusion when, one dark evening, his followers woke him up from his deep sleep and dragged him out of the city to a derelict farm where he witnessed two goat sheds burning. Even the Christian kingdom of Leon Castile would never have conceived such an atrocity! How could they do it?! How could they resort to such an act of terrorism: the systematic assassination of long bearded goats?! An attack on them was a symbolic attack on every man and woman who believed in the Long Beard. The sheikh took drastic measures: he ordered his followers to scour the countryside and find every

---

[35]   See 'On the Free Will of Goats', H. Malik, *BSOAS*, (2003).

long bearded goat, take it home and adopt it as his own. Nothing would ever be the same. This was war.

In the late summer, when the heat could boil a man's brain, the illustrious Sheikh Majd ed-Deen sent a letter, which I have had the fortune to view and copy out; it read:[36]

Peace be to the one who follows guidance

It has been made clear to me that you and your party of heretic bandits will not even allow goats to rest during the night. Far from having a civilised discourse with us, you insult our person in the most horrific manner; this despite the fact that you are my kinsman, my uncle, my grandfather, my sisters' cousin etc. The ocular proof has been found! The terror of the goats speaks for itself. We demand

---

[36] See 'A Post Marxist Oriental Text in a Neo-Hegelian Italy under the Medici Family: A Deconstructionist Feminist Critique', Francois Wilbert, *Anthropological Quarterly*, Issue 1, (1978), for a close reading of the two texts that were so instrumental in the politics of Italian reunification and the reformation. Wilbert points out that Napoleon was forced to land in Egypt three hundred years later to take these two documents back. Napoleon unwittingly changed the course of history for relying on bad intelligence. He thought they were stored in the Library of Alexandria. The discovery that the library had been burnt down a long time ago (before the birth of Christ) upset him greatly. He blamed it on the lack of intelligence that was available to him. Thus, he commissioned the best of French intelligentsia to document and map Egypt; this led to two developments. One, modern Egyptology and two, the realization that good intelligence was required in a military campaign. His reforms bore fruit: upon discovering intelligence that the two documents were actually in a hidden closet in the Winter Palace in St Petersburg he marched his army to get hold of it, only to be defeated by the harsh Russian winter and the battle of Austerlitz. See the marvellously enlightening book on the subject *Tolstoy's War and Peace: a Long Beard Revolution or a Call for Feminist Revolution?*, Jenny Greer, Oxford, (1976).

that you hand over the perpetrators of the burnt shed, otherwise I see no option but to show you overwhelming force in the name of Infinite Justice and Truth. If you do not hand over the perpetrators that make mothers and daughters quiver in fear at the steps of my mosque and residence by the following Friday, I will see no option but to wreak havoc and justice upon you and your party. God shall decide which one of us are truthful. God will give Justice to those Goats slain! God will give Justice.

Yours etc.,

The illustrious and magnificent Sheikh Majd ed-Deen bin Abdullah As-Siyaasi bin Faruuq as-Siyaasi bin Ahmad as-Siyaasi bin 'Arif as-Siyaasi bin Zaheer as-Siyaasi bin Kelbi as-Siyaasi bin Himari as-Siyaasi bin Umar as-Siyaasi bin Ubayd as-Siyaasi bin Adil bin Siyaasi.

The letter was delivered to Sheikh Nur ed-Deen within fifteen minutes by express courier to emphasize the seriousness of his cause. Subsequently, he too composed an appropriate response. After ten minutes, and much deliberation, he delivered it to the courier.

Peace be on the one who follows true guidance

We and my followers do not claim responsibility for this act. We have no knowledge of this and demand evidence that links us to the burning of the two goat sheds that occurred two nights ago, thirty-seven minutes past the hour of two. We know nothing of this. However, we do applaud the brave who committed this feat. Anything that furthers the down fall of this imposition of heretical opinion will always be welcome. As for us, should you dare to make preparation against our person then rest assured that an adequate and equal response will be meted out.

Yours etc.,

*The humble establisher and proof of the Faith Sheikh al-ʿalamma
Nur ed-Deen bin Faruuq as-Siyaasi bin Majd ed-Deen bin Adil bin
Siyaasi bin Umar as-Siyaasi bin Ahmad as-Siyaasi bin ʿArif as-Siyaasi
bin Zaheer as-Siyaasi bin Kelbi as-Siyaasi bin Himari as-Siyaasi.*[37]

It has been related to me, from Anas bin Kelb bin Kelb bin Jahsh,
that he was present in both sheikhs' rousing speeches which were,
in their essence, lessons in eloquence and form. No surprise then,
that the multitudes gathered to hear these pinnacles of glorious
eloquence; it was as if the very King Alfonso of Castile himself
were descending upon Andalusia to cause havoc and rapine such
was the consternation. Indeed, the speeches of the two sheikhs
aroused such fervour amongst the masses that many were ready
to fight to the very death for what they believed in. 'If a house is
divided against itself, it cannot stand,' some shouted. The whole
city rang out with the hard, brave words such as 'either you are
with us, O brother, or you are against us'. Fists were clenched,
hairy broad chests were proudly displayed and beaten and then,
as was the custom of Siyasa, combed.

It was glorious to see the lights of Siyasa exclaim words of
such eloquence, that they harked back to the old days of the
ancient Arabs when these fratricidal blood lettings resulted in
glorious deeds committed. Nay! Nay! I am at a loss! I am at a loss
to express these vistas, these visions. I am at a loss to convey to
you in ink what these words actually meant to the crowds. Nor
does it seem appropriate for me to convey them in verse, and I

---

[37]   As the reader can see, both are related to each other, but the exact
genealogy is hard to establish. [Trans. note]

am not a bad poet at that! I shall illustrate their eloquence by way of a similitude or parable in the hope that perhaps a sense or a hint of their eloquent scent will gently sooth the readers' nostrils. Their speech, then, was like that of a choice rich Valencian golden nugget of turd that had once fallen from its orifice, hot and steaming in the dark brown earth, immediately fertilising the dead earth bringing forth verdant grass and dandelions, consumed by all in the animal kingdom, even by various species of our canine brothers.

Thus, dear reader, at the beginning of the war, brother was turned against brother, uncle gnashed his teeth against uncle's sister's father's brother, sister against cousin and so forth. The city was in glorious tumult and intellectual fervour. Apparently, everywhere you walked you could see men and women debating about this universally important question.

AN ELUCIDATION ON THE OUTBREAK OF THE SIYASAN WAR AND THE ARRIVAL OF AL-HOMSI

Glory be to Him who has created the Universe and all that is in it to create a Pleonastic Platonic neo-physical triangle of a square in a world ruled by the Manichean forces of Good and Evil and placed me in the in between world of the philosophy of the observer! Although I myself did not witness this war, for I arrived too late, it has been related to me by a very reliable source of great authority, Zaid bin Khaldun bin Jahsh bin Jahsh bin Jahsh bin Kelbi, when I was buying some meat from him, that when the time for handing over the perpetrators expired, there was a period of two weeks when both parties were in a stalemate,

inspecting carefully each other's strengths and weaknesses.
It must have been a sight to watch these men of short and long
beards pass each other in the market, eyeing one another in
vehemence and brotherly enmity! Glory be to Him! But let not
the reader think that both sides did not know how to proceed, nor
that they lacked the will power, for the reader should remember
that both scholars had waged a deadly desert war in the heart
of Arabia. The stalemate was broken by the commander of the
plentiful Long Beards. Sheikh Majd ed-Deen struck the first
blow. Many of his intelligence services, namely two long bearded
Siyasans sitting beneath a tree, had been watching Ilhaam, one
of the top lieutenants of Sheikh Nur ed-Deen. They had reason
to believe that it was he who was responsible for the outrages
against the goat shed and they plotted to eliminate him.

Ilhaam was one of the top lieutenants of the Short Beard
Party, a man of standing, a man of experience, a man of
escapades. Ilhaam, whose profession was goat herder, was an
ascetic and zealous convert to the cause. He applied stringently
the law on himself and on the goats. He took on the arduous
task of trimming the beard of his fifty goats every day; no one
could find fault in him nor question his piety. His piety reached
such great heights that he would not pray behind anyone, before
he measured their beard and, if necessary, trim it down to
length. But his most distinctive characteristic was undoubtedly
that of action. He had been one of the core members who were
instrumental in kidnapping several long bearded goats and
trimming them. One of his most daring escapades that Zaid bin
Khaldun and I still chortle over, when savouring some delicious
goat cheese, was the time when Ilhaam shaved *en masse* a

hundred goats in one single night, next to the very mosque of
Sheikh Majd ed-Deen! I cannot but be amazed by it! Such was
his expertise that not a single hair was longer or shorter than the
obligatory requirement. It can only be one of those miracles that
is bestowed on the friends of God.

When the charges of burning the goat shed was laid against
him, he and his party denied it and made a point by point rebuttal
of the accusation. Nevertheless, the Long Beardists expected the
rebuttal: all they wanted was a reason, a cause to eliminate him.
Once the rebuttal of their accusation came, the second stage was
initiated; namely, the arrival of Yusuf al-Mawsuli on to the steps
of Mosque number four. Yusuf had been informed by his spies
that Ilhaam was praying there. Yusuf in disguise, asked Ilhaam
to explain his doctrines in order for him to be converted. Ilhaam
launched into a tirade on the Long Beardists and what ensued
was that Yusuf, enraged, dealt a heavy blow upon the right eye
of Ilhaam and, grabbing a wooden stool, bashed him on his
unusually small cranium. Yusuf was subsequently chased out of
the place of worship. This was the first blood spilt in this war.

Understandably, when Sheikh Nur ed-Deen heard of the
outrage, he was livid. With a face like a mad barking dog, he
prayed for pestilence on all the Long Beards' houses. To his
congregation, he quoted numerous Siyasan traditions and
provided countless evidences that the Hour was upon us and that
Yusuf al-Mawsuli was the awaited Antichrist. He concluded by
declaring Holy War. The Long Beardists, hearing these libelous
accusations, responded with a treatise now famous and copied:
'On the 99 Proofs that Ilhaam is the awaited Antichrist and the
Necessity of Killing the Poor Dog and its Obligation on every

Muslim male.'[38] The problem with the treatise was the name;
it confused the Siyasans greatly. The resultant effect was that
everyone in the small town went around killing dogs for a whole
week, believing that it was their religious duty. Thus, much to
the dislike of its author, Yusuf, a new treatise was distributed that
read: 'On the 99 Proofs that Ilhaam is the Awaited Antichrist and
the Necessity of his Killing'.

On the appointed day, on the holy day of Friday, the two
parties gathered their strength and arms and met in a field that
to this day is known as the Field of Martyrs, on account of the
death of the Long Beardist, Shujaa' bin Asad bin Kelb bin Kelb
bin Haraam bin Harb and the Short Beardist, Uzayr bin Asad
bin Kelb bin Kelb bin Haraam bin Harb. Not to mention the
numerous goats that were martyred indiscriminately, without
mercy, when a group of Short Beardists grabbed some kid goats
and a large pregnant goat and ascended an oak tree, threatening
to slaughter them if the Long Beardists did not surrender.

I have heard from some erudites at court that it was
comparable to the ancient battles of the Greeks and the Persians,
comparable in deed to a Marathon or perhaps one of the great
battles of the Romans. For the battle was short - exactly two hours
and 35 minutes - but in intensity it was longer than any battle
that man has ever witnessed, at least, in this parallel universe.
It consisted of the customary man-to-man combat, whereby the
best of the two parties fought each other. It was there, on that
bloody plain, that the brothers Shujaa' and Uzayr met, split by a
doctrine that did not recognise kinship bonds. On that field of

---

[38]   The manuscript can now be found in the British Library. It is seen as
a seminal text for Western legal theoreticians. [Trans.]

death, they fought and dealt each other death blows with their sharp pitch forks. Then, the two goats fought: one long bearded, Harb,[39] and the short bearded, Nemir.[40] They fought each other, they parried, they charged, they hurled themselves, until both died of exhaustion. Then, the poets stood in duel and recited verses against each other. Still no result came. And so, it came to pass that the battle began in earnest; it was indeed a bloody glorious mess! Each side shouting to their men: 'forward in the name of God!' Each side launching their primitive tools of war into each other. Each side biting, hacking, gouging, piercing, slicing, and cutting, causing terrible violence on each other's goats. Yusuf al-Mawsuli slaughtered an estimated 20 short bearded goats grazing in nearby fields, causing panic amongst the ranks of the Short beards. A retreat ensued. Suddenly, when the battle seemed lost, out of nowhere the ferocious Sheikh Nur ed-Deen rode into the fray on an armoured bull, causing havoc amongst the Long Beardist.[41] Glory! Glory was seen on the horns

---

[39] War [trans.]

[40] Tiger [trans.].

[41] See *Death in the Afternoon*, E. Hemingway, Garnet, (1934). Hemingway maintained that the origins of bullfighting lay in an ancient Roman tradition, whereby the sacrifice of the bull was an off shoot of the cult of Baal and symbolised the taming of Death by man. However, in *Origins of Spanish Bullfighting*, Fernando Testarossa, Madrid, (1999), disagrees and points out that Sheikh Nur ed-Deen that was the actual founder of bullfighting. There are historical accounts from numerous sources that he had picked the bull and reared it with a view to use it for fighting and surprise. He unknowingly picked the fighting bull strain that presently serves as the model for bullfighting. The bull he picked was strong necked, sharp horned, lean and muscular and was tested and fought with the assistance of Yusuf al-Mawsuli. In fact, Testarossa suggests that the cry 'Ole', which is said once the bullfighter has killed the animal,

of the bull. Men ran holding their rears, men lay on the ground gorged, men screamed for strength. The secret weapon of mass destruction charged with bloodlust, however, ran off, seemingly out of control. He circled the field violently, snorting out his terrible fury, causing probably as much damage to the rider as well as to others in the field. In this way, seventy goats were felled. There was a sort of unstructured chaotic harmony in the whole fighting.

A veteran of the war said that watching Ilhaam riding on his armoured donkey, his sharp goat staff dispatching infinite blows on his dreaded enemies, was a marvellous sight worthy of the poetry of Antara. With sheer force of will, with no care for his life, this one black-eyed warrior charged against the ranks of Yusuf al-Mawsuli. Yusuf, being on foot and commanding the vanguard, had, up to that point, concerned himself only with the safety of Sheikh Majd ed-Deen. But seeing his arch nemesis charge against his men, he broke rank screaming like a wild ferocious donkey. His sheikh, although rearing to go out against the foe, saw his devoted disciple and urged him onward.

'Look men!' the sheikh said, 'there goes stonewall Yusuf. There goes brave Yusuf!'

It was one of the most poetic things he had seen in his life. I have since heard that the clash between the two commanders was something out of the *Iliad*. I believe Yusuf suffered over seventy blows of the goat staff that day and Ilhaam perhaps fifty blows to the head from Yusuf's club. Yet none gave into each other.

---

comes from the time Yusuf was gored in the posterior and shouted out in pain 'Ole'; he was subsequently carried out by the assistants, with the applause of the great sheikh and so the bull was found for the great battle.

The battle could have continued for longer, had it not been for the troops of Sultan Mardanish, whose Greek commander, Abu Ja'far, rode in and stopped the melee. Abu Ja'far separated the parties and immediately instituted martial law for three days, until the famous mediator and philosopher al-Homsi arrived to resolve the dispute.

I have met some of these veterans who took part and all still display their battle wounds proudly to this day. They walk the markets honoured that they were one of those glorious five hundred men that fought each other and lost an ear, a finger and an eye for the noblest of causes. Some, I hear, have even nurtured a grudging friendship with each other, despite their views, because of that glorious battle. These men were never the same after that day. These men were walking martyrs. Although they may not see you, nor hear, nor eat for that matter, they yearn to relive that day, the pinnacle of manhood, when man had his muscular arms around the neck of the beast and slew it, that day of Shujaa' and Uzayr that still lie there alive, amongst the rest of the martyrs, saying only that they have done their duty.

O those halcyon days of yore! Where are you? Glory be to Him who created the Universe in a parallel of lofts stacked one on top of each other, so one does not know where one is, yet one finds such a chaotic harmony in this whimsical and yet so important world, where one is but a player in a mystery play written by a Greek tragedian! Glory be to Him!

Part II

An introduction to the character of al-Homsi, my meeting with him, and what I learnt therein. And his presence and how his favour led to the solving of the Siyasan crisis. And of how my station was raised in the eye of the Sultan of Valencia.

My arrival in Siyasa was fortuitous. Unfortunately I could not, to my eternal regret, have witnessed the momentous events that had just passed in this unassuming little city. However, the hand of Destiny decreed such that my curiosity and my hunger for learning meant that the news of my arrival had spread far and wide in the city. All over the city they pointed my aspect out. In bazaars, street corners, homes, baths, mosques even, the populace talked of that curious stranger who asked and asked and never ceased asking. And with this sole virtue was I, Ibn Fudayl, ushered into the presence of this most profound man, Jamal ed-Deen al-Homsi, of whom this fantastic and yet so humble history is about.

It had come to pass, that the populace knew I too had taught in Damascus, Baghdad and Isfahan. Soon, I was asked to deliver a lecture on the theology of the Mutazzalite School.[42] I was

---

[42] A school of philosophy during the early Abbasid Empire that for a while caused a great deal of controversy amongst jurisprudents and scholars of Islam, until its resolution. [Trans.]

initially reluctant to deliver the lecture for I doubted that these
people could have really understood the wisdom of the East, in
particular my subtle argument that the hypothetical paradigms
of our age are not actually paradigms but hypothetical philology
of lust. In any case, I delivered the lecture with my customary
verve and panache. Like a swordsman, I cut, thrust and dissected
the argument. Like a tiger, I pounced and leaped at the axioms.
Like a champion, I trounced and mocked at the priories so that
some closet-Mutazzalites quivered in fear saying: 'Behold, here is
another Juwayni reincarnated. The harbinger of our destruction
has come!' Other closet-Mutazzalites in hopeful wonder
declared: 'The natural son of Ibn Sina had returned to Andalus!'
And though, as I had expected, the central idea was completely
missed by these Westerners; I was still given a standing ovation
by virtue of its stylistic content and sheer audacity. Further, when
they saw me sporting a beard that was not quite short and not
quite long, it was deemed to be revolutionary by the people. I was
hailed by the people as Siyasa's very own Ibn Rushd and carried
back to my residence on their shoulders. In the following days,
I was asked by both the Long Beardists and the Short Beardists to
deliver my reasoning on such a compromise, because both sides
realised that this war of attrition would lead to further loss of
blood. I prepared the lecture over a series of days and delivered it
in the main square of the city.[43] It was received with astonishment

---

[43] See *Imagined Societies: Reflections on the Origins and the Spread
      of Pseudo-Erotic Nationalisms,* Benedict Anderson, Princeton,
      (1978), and *On Liberty,* Isaiah Berlin, Pinguin, (1967). They have
      both shown how the very expression of enforcing moderation
      is a form of extremism. In the case of Ibn Fudayl's brilliant
      'Middle-Beardian way', as Berlin coined it, became so persuasive

and applause by all. I was hailed a hero yet again! And it seemed that I had, overnight, become a bit of a celebrity in the city. Consequently, my celebrity lead to many doors being opened for me. I was shown places where I could go to cure my incessant migraines that afflicted me more often of late. I was invited to banquets of leaders and elders. I was further raised in the eyes of the people when I showed my humbleness, for they could not believe that I, Ibn Fudayl, scholar, intellectual and philosopher could eat barley bread with an old woman! And in this fashion was I, one evening, ushered into al-Homsi's glorious presence.

I was lead to his humble abode, a small house in the centre of the city, filled with books, scientific equipment, strange contraptions and liquids of various odours and colours. As I entered his presence, I caught him like a praying mantis sitting with other

---

that it was taken on by the state. Ibn Fudayl was subsequently promoted as a result, but the Valencian state misunderstood and corrupted this revolutionary new way and enforced the idea uniformly. Thus, from a relatively free country, you had guards and soldiers on street corners enforcing the length of the beard checking that everyone was uniform in their length. Berlin points out that this concerted effort to enforce liberal Beardism became itself, a sort of tyranny. In the history of Andalusia it was unprecedented that visitors were placed in certain beard growing houses (*Dar Tarbiyat el-Lehya*) where they were forced to grow their beards to the appropriate length or be denied access to the country. Trade was undoubtedly affected, in fact, the down fall of the principality of Valencia was due to a faction of disgruntled peasants who, unable to grow any facial hair due to their albinism, were funded by the Roman Pontificate to revolt. These peasants carried out a twenty-year period of guerrilla warfare that was so draining on the state financially that it led to its collapse. For a detailed discussion on this topic, see *Short Beardista Inspirations, Che Guevara and the Origins of the Iraq War,* Frank Deutscher, Boston, (2006).

dignitaries, several buxom maids, eyeing a piece of venison and fiercely attacking it.[44] As was his custom, he rested his right hand on his somewhat stout stomach, and greeted me heartily saying:

'Ah, my fellow, if (¼=¾) is (¼=¾), then the reason of the unreason, with which my unreason is afflicted so weakens my reason that with reason I murmur and believe in a paradoxical universe of beauty and truth, fortuitous to the one who reflects upon the cosmology of the astronomers. The singular truth of life can be found in the elixir of the philosopher's stone. And ultimate truth is as true as the rectum of a dog! I am from a world of universal paradigms of *parralellular* insular lofts which converted, seems almost metaphorical; yet, I can relate that I am as perpendicularly happy as a Pythagorean to see you!'[45]

---

[44] See 'Foucault, Kafka, The Da Vinci Code, Arab Masculinity and Female Bisexuality: A Deconstructionist Reading', where Dr Volgare asserts that this was a revolutionary move, for al-Homsi completely redrew the gender map in the West. According to her, he should be attributed the title of the first 'male feminist' in the West, not Sylvia Pankhurst or George Eliot. According to Dr Volgare, he dared to treat women on an equal footing breaking the taboos of Iberian society, including them as equals in his famous philosophical banquets. She suggests, he unknowingly introduced to the West the salon culture of France, where the *Enlightenment philosophes* and leading ladies met to discuss ideas current in pre-revolutionary France. It was this willingness to break convention in al-Homsi that led to the French Revolution. See *Philosophes, Oriental Revolutionary Intellectual Antagonist and the Seeds of the French Revolution*, R. Darntan, Vichy, (1992). However, Dr Crowe has critiqued this theory in a lecture entitled 'Oriental Barbarisms', delivered by her at SOAS in 2006; she suggests a new paradigm that al-Homsi had bought these maids for a paltry sum at the Murcian slave market. The lecture has not been accepted by the academic community.

[45] For a biographical note on al-Homsi see Ibn Khallikan's *Biographical Dictionary*, further, see *The Great Philosophers*, R. Scrutom,

And then once he finished he belched heartily as was also his custom.

It was beautiful, I chortled, I breathed anew, I was a new-born babe snatched from the bloody uterus of my mother into al-Homsi's loving arms! I was like the messiah mentioned in the Gospels of the Christians who were cleansed in the river Jordan, I was like the companion of the fish belched back into the world. Verily, I had found him! Finally, I had found him! It was as if only he understood me and I understood him! I did not eat that evening. Mesmerized, I watched him eat, the juice of the venison trickled down his silvery white beard, for I realised there and then that those words were his defining statement - his legacy to the world. They were concise, succinct; no room for ambiguity: simply beautiful. The whole moment, to me, was comparable in magnificence to the trial and execution of Socrates in front of his accusers. Indeed, I myself, heard the visitors to the banquet relate the very same tale to other men and it became a magnificent legend. It had such a clear simplicity that you were decried a fool if you said that it didn't make sense. I was witness to this glorious statement, understood and available to the elect of the elect of humanity that it passed into romantic myth.

Only the foolish, like the buxom women at the table, uttered those blasphemous words 'I do not understand'. Only they dared, but this was in line with the weaker sex's temperament

---

Delphi, (1998). Scrutom cites al-Homsi as being the founder of Postmodernism and an antecedent for Nietzsche. In fact, he goes even further and suggests, contrary to popular belief, that Nietzsche died of syphilis. It is more likely that it was al-Homsi's statement that drove Nietzsche to madness, unreason and ultimately death. But it also helped him to write that momentous masterpiece *The Antichrist* and *Thus Spake Zarathustra*.

and character.[46] And I advise anyone who embarks on the path of wisdom never to enter into discourse with the fair sex on this subject. For at best, it would confuse them and they may fall in to heretical belief. And at worst, it could onset a violent madness of the mind, which may lead them to harm one's own person. For on my own admission, I foolishly embarked on such a discussion with one of the women of my household. I was forced to utter the words 'divorce' three times, on account of me being confined to bed for several days. To this day, do I wear the scars of her inner logic on my forehead: Life, O friend, is a school in itself.[47]

As for the layman that may be perusing this book, I feel that an explanation of these words is in order. The unassuming reader, must understand that there are great controversies surrounding those words, not because of unambiguity but rather for their depth in meaning. He might be forgiven for his bewilderment when he discovers that there are scholars who are in complete apposition in their beliefs concerning the

[46]   For Ibn Fudayl's misogyny, see the wonderful article, 'Oriental Barbarism in Post-Neo Colonial Arab Women's Literature', Valentina Viene, BSOAS, (2002).

[47]   P789, *Post-Modernity in Medieval Spain*, R. S. Fletcher. Fletcher believes that the lasting wound he received from his first wife, when she accidentally dropped a vase on his head, was actually the cause that eventually killed him and also the cause of him writing the book. See Ibn Khallikan's *Biographical Dictionary*, where Ibn Khallikan relates that Ibn Fudayl refused Sultan Ibn Mardanish's Jewish physician and brought in a doctor from Siyasa instead, who treated the gash with bandage and an ointment of Valencian manure which, according to the Jewish physician, made his wounds fester and become infected. Ibn Fudayl became confined to the court of the sultan and remained in this vegetative state for another ten years where, according to other sources, he lectured, married and had three children.

statement. But the secret to the speech is that it is layered on many different levels.

Let me illustrate my point with a real-life similitude. In our day, we have Juwayry bin Wahsh, the philosopher and goat herder: he believes that all the truth in the world can be found in the rectum of a dog. He has taken the literal meaning and, therefore, seeks out or sometimes chases various samples of the canine species in order to find out this truth. The result? He dispatches them from the highest tower found in Valencia's strong fortifications.[48]

In stark contrast to Juwayry, we have al-Badawi, he has taken the metaphorical meaning and believes that the whole universe and the rectum of the dog is one and the same. It has resulted in him carrying around a thin tubular contraption with a finely polished crystal attached to it. This crystal magnifies the object he is peering into many times over. He has attached to this device, a spatula, which he inserts deep into the posterior of his canine friends. Then peers into the darkness of the rectum for further illumination.[49] And from his findings he carries out complex mathematical calculations.[50] He has come up with a remarkable formula that, he claims, will explain everything in the universe. It is as follows:

$$(\tfrac{1}{4}=\tfrac{3}{4}\neq\tfrac{1}{4}=\tfrac{3}{4})=(\S h^{|}\dagger/\hat{o}^{\vee}f)+(f7\ddot{i}>\tfrac{3}{4}\times\tfrac{1}{2})=E=mc^2$$

---

[48] See *An Introduction to Galileo Galilei's Works and Influences*, R. Mandeblum, Scientifica, (1967).

[49] What we moderns would call a telescope or microscope [Trans.].

[50] *See Al-Badawi, An Oriental Precursor to Newtonian and Einsteinian World*, R. Dworkins, Vintage, (2005). See also Karl Popper's discussion of al-Badawi in his wonderful tract *Oriental Paradigms in Western Scientific Study*, Karl Popper, Oxford, (1956).

In conclusion then, should the layman visit Valencia and come by a rather tall man peering into the abyssal posterior of our canine cousins[51] under an oak tree; or, perhaps, should he happen to walk in on a rather wiry bearded man throwing down a yelping host of dogs from the tall towers of the Valencia, making it appear as if it were raining dogs,[52] he should not worry: they are only Juwayry and al-Badawi, giving the world the fruits of al-Homsi's teachings.

There is only one thing left for the laymen to ponder on; what of the belch? Was it a compliment or geniunely part of the text? For, as any linguist will know, the nature of linguistics is such that even the belch can be part of the esoteric language. On the belch, the schools have been split. There are those, like Juwayry, who holds that the belch has no meaning: it was just a rhetorical flourish from the great philosopher. However al-Badawi, who wrote a twelve-volume treatise on just this point, maintains otherwise.[53] He refuses to accept that al-Homsi would simply add the belch without meaning, for al-Homsi did everything with purpose and intention and wanted posterity to take the belch into account. Al-Badawi's book is excellent, though somewhat harsh and scathing. One sees no need for him to denounce the poor lineage of Juwayry and remind the world that his name meant dung beetle and that

---

[51] P232-234, *Al-Badawi, an Oriental Precursor to Newtonian and Einsteinian World*, R. Dworkins. It has been suggested here by Dworkins that Ibn Fudayl was also aware of al-Homsi's theory that all of us descend from one common ancestor.

[52] Hence the expression 'it is raining cats and dogs'. See *The History of the English Language*, Justin McCarthur, University of Texas, (1978).

[53] See *Sharh al-Wadih fee Takri' al-Homsi*, Abu Jamil al-Badawi, Cairo, (1923).

the former was not comely to look at.[54] Neither was there a
need for him to denounce the lineage of his goat, his wife etc.
These scholarly rivalries aside, the book has been the dominant
opinion adopted in the West.[55]

To return to this delicious philosophical banquet, we
found ourselves drawn to each other unwittingly. He would
at first glint his eye at me and ask me questions about my
lineage. He was somewhat disappointed when I rejected
the notion that I was of Aryan descent. However, when he
found out that there might be enough evidence (namely my
green eyes) to suggest that my mother's ancestry might be
of Arcadian origin, he was pleased. For it is believed, my
mother's ancestors settled in Egypt under the Ptolemies.
As the dinner continued, he began asking me more probing
philosophical questions, to which I replied with great finesse

---

[54] P657, *Valencian Manure, Globalisation and the Shaping of Western
Europe*, Caterina Pinto. Whilst it is true that the word means 'dung
beetle', it was really a name given to the scientist by the Sultan of
Valencia, in recognition of his great contribution to the refinement
of Valencian manure. The full title is actually Juwayr ad-Dawla
(dung beetle of the state). The name is not at all derogatory knowing
as we do that Valencia and the rest of the world, at the time, valued
Valencian manure more than gold. We know that Juwayry used it
with pride and never tried to conceal it.

[55] See *Tarikh al Harb bayna al-Juwayriya wa al-Badawiya fee Balancia
ithna Mulk al-Muwahideen*, Al-Kindi, Cairo, (1876); it has actually
been translated by H.A.R. Gibb available to us under the title
*The History of the War Between the Juwayries and the Badawis in
Valencia During the Kingship of the Almohads*, H.A.R. Gibb, Oxford,
(1936). Al-Kindi points out that al-Badawi was mortally wounded
when he led the charge against the barricade held by the party of
Juwayry. Similar riots followed all over the Islamic world such as
Nishapur and Isfahan. The reader should also not forget that the
Paris Commune (1871) was also linked to this controversy.

and verve. For instance, I gave him the circumference of a square in another dimension (my premise being that God could do anything). I too began, to the horror and disgust of his students, questioning him. He was pleased with my flirtatious boldness and replied with wit and passion whilst passing me a cup of fermented grape juice to alleviate my migraine. We talked on many subjects, from alchemy to the circumference of the buxom maids' bosoms and, as my migraine began to alleviate, he began to jest with me. I thought: 'This philosopher king is human after all!'

'Are you a triangular Pythagorean?'

I would reply in similar quick wit:

'No I am an octogenarian stoic.'

We would watch his students write these retorts down in their books whilst others would try to memorise our rapport. Both of us chortled till our bellies hurt in the difficulties that their minds encountered. We were like two lovers entwined in the drunkenness of bucolic fervour!

I believe he had never met someone like me, so quick in philosophic wit and confidence. Likewise, I had never met such a man that uttered profundity, even in jest. That dinner that lasted up until the dawn prayer and led to further intimate meetings, could almost be likened to trysts between two lovers. By the end of these somewhat intellectually sensual meetings, we realised that we were for each other, and I considered myself not merely his disciple, not merely his student, but his intellectual lover and friend - forever. Many a night, would we test and analyse thousand samples of Valencian sheep manure or discuss his most marvellous book: *The Inanimateness of Inanimate Objects in a Free Will World* and in between our intellectual endeavours he would relate to me snippets of his life.[56]

HIS EARLY LIFE

The philosopher's origins are relatively unknown, even by his most intimate companions. Some of his disciples believe that his ancestors descend from Samarqand, whilst others say he was born in Homs or Nishapur. Various myths have been created by those that came after him. As far as I know, nothing mystical has ever occurred to him and he has not indicated anything to that effect to me.

The philosopher was always vague about his childhood, in order that his personality was not confused with his teachings. From the snippets that he has revealed to me, I can only hypothesize that he displayed, from an early age, an appetite for knowledge and that as a result he suffered. His family could not bear his incessant craving for knowledge. Thus, he was passed on from family member to family member, institution to institution until he left home to quench his thirst. He has related that most of his youth and manhood was spent in pursuing his studies. He is a master of many tongues and subjects, including Greek, Latin, Indian tongues, grammar, rhetoric, mathematics, alchemy, astronomy, philosophy and jurisprudence.

However, the road to knowledge was never smooth. He lost a hand, was robbed by bandits and was refused entry to numerous cities on account of his profession. Eventually his great genius was recognised. When he reached the full flower of his

---

[56]   Now lost. During the Third Reich, Hitler ordered that all the copies be collected and burnt for fear that it would expose him as the awaited Nosferatu. [Trans.]

manhood,[57] his intellectual capacities matured and his words took on an eloquence that gained him access to the finest institutions that the civilised world has ever witnessed. Every sultan has heard of his repute or listened to a lecture of his. He himself has related that the very generous and noble Sultan Salah ed-Deen al-Ayyubi provided him with an escort of a hundred guards, to shepherd him to the borders of his empire and on towards North Africa. However, it was not until he reached Andalusia that his ideas took on a greater prominence.[58] After several letters of introduction and delivering of lectures, he was hailed a genius and received a considerable stipend from the Sultan of Valencia, an avid patron of the arts, who surrounded himself with the finest minds that world had ever seen. There he began teaching on statecraft and the nature of the viscosity of Valencian faeces in the light of Plotinus and Xenophanes.[59]

HIS CONTRIBUTION TO CHEMISTRY AND THEOLOGY

I do not wish here to explain all of his teachings for fear of doing them a great injustice. The reader, if he is interested in his

---

[57] Literally 'his scrotum was filled with blood'. I translated the intention of the author here to clear up any ambiguity. [Trans.]

[58] See *Moorish Spain*, R. Fletcher, Phoenix, (1998). Fletcher suggests that after the fall of the Umayyads, Andalusia split up into various smaller kingdoms, which all sought legitimacy for their rule. It meant that many of these rulers would patronise the arts to further their aims in achieving legitimacy. Hence artists and intellectuals from all the corners of the world would flock to Andalusia during this period. The period, also known as '*asr al-muluk at-tawa'if* or the Age of the Party Kings, was one of the most creatively fruitful periods in the history of the Iberian Peninsula.

[59] See *Oriental Undertones in Clauswitz and American Modern Statecraft*, William Oppenheimer, Chicago, (1999).

teachings, should refer to the *Sharh* for that.[60] But I have seen
with my very own eyes the effect his knowledge and learning
has had on the world at large. Al-Homsi did not believe that
knowledge belonged to one people or faith and was therefore
liberal in distributing his pearls of his knowledge and wisdom.

It came to pass that whilst studying and preparing a joint
paper on 'The Similarities and the Dissimilarities of the Frankish
Species' for the University of Valencia, he received an invitation
from Father Santiago, the head of the Monastery of St James
in the Christian kingdom of Asturias. The Abbey wanted the
philosopher's assistance in creating a fermented grape solution
that alleviated all sorts of ailments.

Father Santiago had been instrumental in unifying the
Iberian Peninsula under the Catholic orthodoxy.[61] Through
heavy preaching and threats of eternal damnation, he
extinguished amongst many of our Christian brethren the old

---

[60]   He refers to his own work *As-Sharh al-Fadil lil-faylasuf al-Kamil*,
       this work has been lost but the work is mentioned by historians such
       as as-Sibti in their histories.

[61]   P124, *A History of the Church*, B. Graham, SMC, (1998). The Council
       of Nicaea of 325, modern day Iznik in Turkey, the Church decided
       on official doctrine as being: *'I believe...in one Lord Jesus Christ,
       the only begotten Son of God, begotten of his Father before all the
       worlds, God of God, Light of Light, Very God of Very God, begotten,
       not made, being of one substance with the Father, by whom all things
       are made. Who for us men, and for our salvation, came down from
       Heaven, and was incarnate by the Holy Ghost of the Virgin Mary, and
       was made man, and was crucified also for us under Pontius Pilate.
       He suffered and was buried, and the third day he rose again according
       to the scriptures, and ascended into heaven, and sits at the right hand
       of the Father. And He shall come again in glory to judge both the quick
       and the dead; whose kingdom shall have no end.'* This is known as the
       Nicene Creed.

doctrine of Arianism that had pervaded throughout the East and
the peninsula.[62] But old ways do not die out that easily. Arianism
had not quite died out in parts of the Iberian Peninsula and this
was to cause a great deal of problems in the minds of the people,
as we shall soon see.

Al-Homsi, whilst being a superb theologian, did not delve
in to matters of creed. He deemed it sufficient that the common
folk needed mystical superstitious beliefs in order to live a moral
and virtuous life. For how else could the layman understand the
intangible mystery that is the Being? Thus miracles, ritual, and
many other aspects found in faith had to be instituted simply to
aid the laymen in understanding the intangible and so did not
meddle into the affairs of the heart. However, for the elect, the
plea of ignorance was simply not enough. One needed to be like
the philosopher king, who could reach closeness to the Eternal
by perceiving the truth through the trigonometrical eye of the
mind divided by the cosine. And though he scoffed at these
theologians for holding philosophically preposterous beliefs and
left them to graze in the field of ignorant serenity, he still managed
to make, perhaps, one of the greatest contribution to this noble
art of theology. For he created, somewhat inadvertently, the

---

[62]   P234. In *A History of the Church*, B. Graham says of Bishop Arius
of Alexandria (250-336CE) and his followers that they rejected the
Nicene Creed vis-à-vis the official church. Bishop Arius believed
that only the Father was God and Jesus was subordinate, created and
not eternal. His teachings, however, were deemed heretical because
it rejected the Trinitarian conception of God. Consequently, he was
exiled by Emperor Constantine, his followers were persecuted for
their beliefs. His teachings, nevertheless, spread to parts of Italy,
Gaul and Spain. A similar story can also be said of the Syrian monk
Nestorius (d.451).

noblest sacred wine that the Church had ever tasted. The wine converted thousands to the faith of the Christians, on account of the wonderful taste of the wine of the Eucharist.[63]

As for me, admittedly, my reasons were less altruistic than my master's. I was most eager to aid him in this medical experiment. I hoped, thereby, that the concoction could perhaps alleviate my incessant migraines that forced me in to the licentious dens of ill repute, in order that I may access my prescription. Thus, the prospect of concocting such a magnificent medicine excited me; it meant that I had access to a more wholesome environment. Thus, we eagerly left Siyasa, galloping into the sunset as fast as we could on our two donkeys towards Asturias.

---

[63] P124, *A History of the Church*. St Paul instituted this rite involving the eating of unleavened bread and drinking blessed wine. It is taken from the Lord's Supper where Jesus and his disciples, in anticipation of his crucifixion, took part in celebrating Passover. The Jews celebrate Passover by slaughtering a lamb because it commemorates their deliverance from the clutches of the Pharaoh. Similarly the Christians, following the teachings of St Paul, eat symbolically the body of Jesus, i.e. 'the lamb of God', and drink his blood in order to remember their deliverance from sin. Though this was considered blasphemous in Jewish teachings since blood was forbidden, St Paul, paving a new way, believed that Jesus had instructed his disciples to symbolically drink his blood and eat his flesh. It is not clear, however, if this was the case, since all the gospels were written after Paul and may have been influenced by his teachings. In any case, it is believed that this rite was not practised by any of the disciples and was a personal inspiration to Paul. The term Eucharist is a replacement of the 'Lord's Supper' because of the early Church Fathers' consternation that the rite was too similar to the mystery cults in the region, for example, the cult of Osiris, Mithra and Dionysus where all the Egyptian, Persian and Hellenic gods died for the sins of mankind and their flesh was consumed in order that Man might gain eternal life through them.

The journey to the Kingdom of Asturias was an arduous one and took us nearly three weeks. The journey, in truth, should have taken two weeks, however, the extra week was due to the eccentric and yet amazing things that I saw in my teacher. The journey allowed me to watch the old man closely in all aspects of his behaviour. I found his comportment peculiar and yet refreshing, for he was a man who was completely out of this world, so much so that he forgot sometimes even to adhere to the most basic rudiments of etiquette or hygiene. I was astonished, it was as if he had not known a mother or a father or had been a foundling raised amongst the carrion eaters of the Arabian desert. He reminded me of Socrates, one, who disdained cleanliness due to his deep penetrative thought and otherworldliness.

I remember, once, after having devoured several whole wild chickens that he had captured close to a farm, and drunk several of my prescriptive bottles of fermented grapes all by himself, he felt the pangs of fecal extraction. I watched him as he betook himself to a bush where he remained uttering indescribable groaning and other noises related to answering the call of nature. Excited by the philosophical groanings, I too edged closer to the bush in order to study his flatulent uttering further, for one never knows when wisdoms drop by. And as I peered in suddenly, his face became arrested and contorted. His whole body shook and he remained in this state for many moments. When he did not return, I decided to edge even closer to investigate this remarkable phenomenon. I perceived that a thought had entered his head. He was just like Socrates the Athenian, wrestling with his primordial state of being! Is not this one Pindaric universe beautiful? At any time does the muse whisper! The idea had diverted him so much that he was transfixed on that spot for a day and a night and nothing came out of him. I remained by his side and watched as if I were one of those astonished Greeks who gathered around the great Socrates to gaze his feat of mental and physical will as he pondered.

In my humble opinion, I would suggest that al-Homsi's position in terms of physical endurance was far more difficult than Socrates's, since he had betaken to squatting and could not distribute his weight evenly on both his legs, causing one of them to swell up.

That long drama worthy of a being a Homeric epic, induced in him several symptoms: firstly, his face contorted itself into a purple reddish colour, as if he were struggling in extracting the thought inside him. Secondly, a cramp developed in his exposed hind legs and the region thereabouts due to his squat position, the bitter cold biting and consequently freezing parts of his exposed anatomy.[64] At one point, when it became extremely cold, I must confess I saw no option but to rub hot olive oil ointment everywhere to alleviate his mental thought processes. On the second day, I awoke frightened for myself, as his fruit came out of him with a great thunderous and glorious roar. I thought, at first, that it may have been a bear, but I was soon calmed by the pungent odour reminiscent of Valencian manure; it was just the sheikh up to his knees in the glorious mess that his mind had created. I received him gladly and was overjoyed that all he had suffered for his intellectual endeavours was just

---

[64] See Ibn Khallikan's *Biographical Dictionary*. Al-Homsi was not survived by anyone, and the journey to the Asturias may have been the reason. See *Il Coglione di al-Homsi*, Caterina Pinto, Napoli, (1999).

mild frostbite around his cahoones. We tarried a while, regaining some strength, before continuing on our journey. I padded the saddle with soft cushions and insisted on treating his malady with hot olive oil every evening, but alas he never fully recovered.

The monastery of Montepulsiano was perched precariously on a crag of rock. We were received heartily by Father Santiago who offered us all of his courtesy and piety. We were housed in one of the spacious rooms at the monastery and were provided with all the different and tasty delicacies that Christian hospitality and charity could afford.

The very next day, Father Santiago offered us a tour of the monastery and the surrounding hills where the legendary grape, said to be the finest on earth, was cultivated. Being single minded men of determination, we refused this leisurely tour and began our work in earnest. For three days and three nights, we did not leave our laboratory. We took very little to eat and were attended to by a monk, Adolphius by name, who shared our scientific hopes and endeavours, pushing the very bounds of medicine and chemistry. On the third day, we emerged victorious having gone beyond the frontiers that no sane human being would venture. We had, under intense pressure, concocted and tasted various fermentations of grape solutions and did not stop until we had found the perfect medicinal fermented grape solution that we named Venito. Venito was unique because it was correct in chemical consistency, colour and taste.[65] It was the red nosed Adolphus who declared it a

---

[65] P567. *A History of the Church*, 'a casket of which was sent to the Pope Onorio III (1216-1227), who was so pleased with the wine that he asked for a cutting and set about cultivating the wine in Tuscany. He named the village that cultivated the wine after the

blinding success. After tasting our now famous medicine, he let out a chain of pious exclamations; we knew then that we had arrived at the right solution.[66]

However, the pious exhortations of brother Adolphius triggered off a chain of events that caused a cataclysm in the Christian Iberia. Adolphius's refrains awakened in the philosopher, perhaps, a faint memory of childhood illumination. Thus al-Homsi, red nosed, with a bottle in his left hand staggered out of the magnificent wine cellar declaring to the whole world that He, the Son, was a *Natural Child*,[67] and the Holy Ghost was actually one and the same, for his Father was a separate platonic entity whilst the *Rex*[68] was his true Father - he was the *philo*,[69] and had been the shadow in his life, because he begat him in the cupboard with his mother - the *sophia*.[70] Whilst the father was out he, Rex, had wrestled with

---

monastery of Montepulsiano. The wine is now one of the most prized wines in Italy.'

[66] P580 *Ibid*. He was the founder of the Adolphian heresy in Spain and Southern France. Although the heresy died out in Spain, later popes were forced to conduct crusades against Southern France in order to bring the populace back into Roman Catholicism (i.e. the Albigensian crusade).

[67] This section is extremely difficult to translate due to its ambiguity. [Trans.]

[68] Rex here can mean many things: King, Lord or Tyrannosaurus Rex.

[69] Some Jewish historians have attributed al-Homsi to being a follower of Philo, the Hellenized Jew who was enraptured with Greek ideas and is thought to have introduced Platonic ideas like the *Logos* in to the Old Testament.

[70] Some Armenian nationalists have claimed that al-Homsi's mother was Armenian by the name Sophia. This has fuelled further calls of independence from Turkish oriental despotism. See *The Times*, issue 2789, Jan 25 1989. [Trans.]

her and combined in order to create *philosophia-Io sono della philosophia*.[71] The mother's explanation to his father had been that there were ghosts in the cupboard and that she had gone to investigate when she was possessed.

Adolphius heard these words and was completely amazed. For he believed that al-Homsi, who was by now sleeping deeply on the cold stone floor of the wine cellar, had just explained in the most succinct form possible the secrets of doctrine. He searched for a feather or reed pen, but so excited was he that he failed to write down the words comprehensibly. Thus, he imparted it to his strong memory and set off to the Kingdom of Aragon.

On the authority of al-Kindi's *Tarikh*, the young monk, without allowing himself any rest from his scientific exertions, headed with utmost speed towards the Kingdom of Aragon, on the only mule that *Montepulsiano* possessed. He arrived in the capital of Aragon, Saragossa, within a week dusty and weary but in high spirits. He had ridden day and night, fortified only by the miraculous medicinal properties of the fermented grapes that al-Homsi had created. He gained immediate audience to the august Archbishop of Aragon, Ferdinand el-Rey Lobo, after presenting him with a casket of al-Homsi's medicine. Adolphius excitedly related from memory what he had heard and understood; the

---

[71]   'I am philosophy' [Trans.], this is an extremely ambiguous statement
       yet also very fruitful. It has led Freidrich Heinrich Jacobi, the great
       German philosopher (1743-1819), to conclude that 'the human being
       has such a choice, this single one: nothingness or a God. Choosing
       nothingness, he makes himself into a God, it is impossible that man
       and everything which surrounds him is not merely an apparition. I
       repeat: God is, and is outside of me, living being, existing in itself,
       or I am God. There is no third'. See on *The Evolution of Homsian
       Philosophical Thought*, Albert Webster, Chicago, (2005).

ghost begat the son who lived in a cupboard and that the king was really the father of the ghost and the son was really the king!

The proposition was at first received apprehensively by many of the clerics. Murmurs passed round the cold stone audience room. Many thought the young friar a fool and wanted to give him a good thrashing. Some, like the Franciscan Father Martinez el-Salvatori, a friend and fellow philosopher of the Sapphic School of Emanations, became further confused by Adolphius's frantic utterings and stayed awake further into the night than usual, filled with much uncertainty and disquiet.[72] Father Martinez himself related to me that he did not dare ask for further clarification on the subject and had instead prayed to the Lord that he be given more clarification. In contrast, Archbishop Ferdinand was so delighted by the medicine of al-Homsi, that in an instant Adolphius was made into a cardinal and demanded that the monastery come under his careful supervision. And thus, he gave tacit approval to Adolphius's ideas.

However, as Father Martinez related to me without any bombast or boast, the Spanish Church did not take on the Adolphian doctrine until he, Father Martinez himself, had explained it.

Father Martinez, a Benedictine monk, a most virtuous man, was in the habit of regularly visiting houses of ill repute in order to reform and counsel the ladies for living such licentious lives of sin and debauchery. He often urged them to be generous in charity towards Mankind so that the Lord return their sweet kindnesses. Of course, the pious harlots responded in the best

---

[72]   He was probably a follower of Ibn Bajjah (Avempace) a precursor to Ibn Rushd (Averroes).

way they could to express their piety. It came to pass that on one of these nights of intense sermonizing, Father Martinez found himself hiding in the cupboard. For the Benedictine father had lined up each and every lady of ill-repute in the lobby and had been inspired by the Holy Spirit that these women were in need of all embracing salvation. He cried tears of sadness and joy as he realised that these women carried the stains of dissolution and profligacy and needed utter purification from the clutches of the Devil. However much he disliked it, it required him to baptize each and every sinner, every single one of them! Apart, of course, from the wrinkly old Madame who ran the bordello (she was deemed to be beyond salvation). The baptizing had gone very well until there was a knock on the door. Father Martinez, soon discovered, that the very Archbishop of Saragossa, his pious Excellency Ferdinand el-Rey Lobo, was standing at the door, ready to spread Love and Forgiveness to all of Humanity and offer this fallen house his comforting beneficence. Father Martinez became troubled since he was in a state of naked ablution and not properly attired to face the Archbishop, even if one was doing the Lord's work. Therefore, he asked one of the harlots, Esmeralda, a dark haired fine buxom maid of six and twenty, of whom I have had the pleasure of conversing with and examining, to hide him in the cupboard. She duly complied with his request. Whilst the Archbishop proceeded with his task, the friar discovered a bundle of towels in the cupboard wherein he was hiding. The bundle turned out to be a young child and after the Archbishop had relieved himself of his mighty and glorious beneficence, the Father Martinez emerged and demanded to know who this beautiful bundle of joy was.

According to Father Martinez, of whom I have had the pleasure to accompany in his altruism, Esmeralda, the mother, shrugged and explained how the child had been fathered by the King of Aragon. Father Martinez, exclaimed a 'hallelujah'. The Holy Spirit had explained everything to him. Adolphius had been right after all! Esmeralda added further credence to Adolphius's theory that the house was considered haunted. The Truth had been revealed to him.

The next day, the Benedictine friar left through the back entrance with the child and headed straight to the Archbishop who granted him an audience once he was informed that Father Martinez knew of his nocturnal pieties. Father Martinez related to him the whole story and held aloft the child. Both were astonished at the boy and immediately sought out the king of Aragon and showed him the fruit of his loins. King Alfonso II was pleased, for it was a great achievement that a family who were once provincial noblemen should have a living deity born in one's own house. The king without delay, sent out a royal proclamation announcing that the child was from his own loins. Likewise, the Archbishop, without more ado, sanctified Esmeralda who, out of piety, could now bestow her blessings and forgiveness to anyone who deserved it - without payment. And so, the proselytizing began.

Al-Homsi and this humble writer, once mere spectators in this theatre of human endeavour, entered the arena and played their quiet little roles. We were sent for all the way from the monastery of *Montepulsiano.* And according to the customs of the Kingdom of Aragon, we were knighted and duly vested with barbaric and strange garbs and honoured for several days by the kingdom.

We enjoyed all the pleasures and conveniences that the kingdom offered and taught them many new ideas that fortified their simple minds for many centuries to come.

I remember how al-Homsi advised the King to lend money to the Sultan of Valencia, who was a rather cash strapped sultan, at a rate of interest that was double the amount borrowed. This would mean that when the sultan failed to make repayments or find it a burden to repay the loans, he would be forced to either borrow more money or could give him pieces of land to pay off his debts. Thereby, the kingdom could enrich itself and grow more virtuous! Marvellous! The king thought the plan an ingenious idea and literally begged al-Homsi to become one of his advisers and offered him many many sacks of gold. Al-Homsi, however, was a principled man and, with a swish of the hand, refused. Here I, as his faithful friend, student, nay devotee, stepped in. I urged him to reconsider the king's proposal. I grabbed him by his beard and pointed out that with this wealth he could be wholly self-sufficient and live the life of an ascetic forever! He refused, I twisted the points of his mustachio (a thing that pleased him exceedingly) and said that, if he wished, he could travel the world for wisdom. He refused. But I persisted by painting a picture of great verbal beauty so that al-Homsi could perceive the stucco house perched on the green hillocks of Valencia. I encouraged him to touch the vine growing on its trellises, to feel the roses resting on its off-yellow roman pillars, smell the jasmine adorning the arches and the apple blossoms floating in the air, whilst the soothing trickle of the fountain brought him solace from the obscene world outside. I showed him the sheer practicality of having a lyceum of sorts, independent from the patronage of sultans where he could be like a cynic, stoic, and hedonist of Greece and wander amongst its olive groves, discussing that most important matter of re-educating the fair sex on the new educational principles. In short, he could be like the philosopher king who received the sultans, kings and paupers and would not disdain to receive even the fickle minded: the fair sex and young handsome youths. Alas! It was not to be, he refused to succumb to hypocrisy, to decadence and sloth: he was a man of principle. Giving me a glance of rebuke, he addressed the king saying that he was still under the services of the Sultan of Valencia and could not possibly take up another whilst under his current patron. Such was the gem of his wisdom that the king began to rise up from his seat in front of his newly found teacher. Al-Homsi, however, would tell him that this form of respect was contemptible, the best respect shown to a teacher was the application of the knowledge that the tutor had taught. In the end, Alfonso II applied the lessons effectively; so effectively that al-Homsi always said that only Alfonso, the king of Aragon, had shown him true respect.

Following my attempt at seducing him with eloquent visions of worldly wealth, he withdrew himself from me. I do not wish to paint my master to be a vindictive or angry fellow, rather, with the benefit of hindsight, I have come to realise that he did this out of pure Neo-platonic love. And as much as it pained me, it must have pained him too, though he did not show it. At the dining table his tone of voice possessed a lonely distance that hurt me. At the bath house, when I touched his shoulder in affection and offered to scrub his back, he became uncomfortable and distanced himself. At the library, when I asked him a question, instead of answering the question himself, he referred me to a silly book written by some fool of monk from Cluny. For three days, he avoided my gaze and I retired to bed devoid, empty, alone and torn.

In life, dear reader, I have suffered many hardships and humiliations, I have nearly been shipwrecked off the coast of Sicily, become destitute eating wild grass and berries for days, I have nearly become the evening dinner of the Rus, a species of Viking, a savage cannibal tribe with horrendous table manners that worship a black crow and a man with big hammer they call the thunder God. I have escaped the evil clutches of squinty eyed yellow bandits and dacoits, I have repelled the advances of the unhygienic but attractive women of Gaul, I have flirted with cunning dancing girls, eunuchs and princesses, I have had verbal intercourse with genies and verbal jousts with poets. I have escaped townships at night, forded rivers dodging the poisoned darts of the ferocious Umbongo[73] tribes men close to Sudan, I have cuts, stitches, bruises from my endeavours and still, in comparison, dear reader, those three days were the most difficult period of my life and I will never forget it. But in this way, he taught me the most important lesson no man should forget: the wise man scorns prestige. And yet, to quote an old proverb of Siyasa: *'Every man has a mother who is related to his son and cousin.'*[74] And so, on the third day, expecting another

---

[73]   The Umbongo tribe, a tribe brought into, to use Ernest Renan's phrase, 'the light of history' when the British stumbled upon them. It seems, though, that the tribe had more contact with the outside world than previously believed.

[74]   The passage outside of its context does not have any meaning whatsoever. No references are made of it in the great books on

day of torment, I went to greet him and was taken aback. When he received me with his usual loving warmth, my happiness was restored! So indeed does the universe of the parallel ornithology play the prankster! What was more, my happiness was further increased when he said with his devilish smile that the king's generous offer was to go instead to me, Ibn Fudayl!

To return from this aside, according to al-Kindi, the consequences of this edict was enormous in the Christian kingdom. For the more conservative bishops in the kingdom accustomed, as they were, to the Council of Nicaea and Ephesus, could not accept such a doctrine, despite Adolphius's claim that it was not in contradiction to any of what had come before. These bishops sent out secret messengers who risked their very limbs to petition Rome against such unorthodox views. The king, naturally, was greatly angered by this and viewed this communication as open treachery. Consequently, many a bishop was martyred for his cause.

And here, yet again, al-Homsi stepped in! He reasoned that their lives had already been decreed by the Namer of the Named One of Destiny. I mean here, by the Namer of the Named One, that the One who has been Named is not actually not *named* by Destiny, rather he has been transposed. And since one does not know one's destiny of orthodontic artistry of forms, logically one is forced, if one can use that term, to follow a sort of paradoxical free will of the Namer: a Namer which is unknown, compared to the *Named*

Andalusian proverbs, nor do the great philologists of the Arabic language mention it; the Hagarists, Michael Cook *et al.* gloss this phrase over for it picks out great holes in their theories. Although the phrase is replete with meaning, it can be loosely translated as 'every cloud has a silver lining'. [Trans.]

One's secret, the *secret* that is at the same time desirous to know what its name is in the light of the record that has been produced by the producers of the artists appropriately *Named* Destiny's Child. Therefore, since these and many other clerics were already destined to die, it was better to make this process a smooth one for them, so that they could join the Essence of Being of the Universe.

Al-Homsi devised a marvellous contraption that dispatched these poor creatures to the afterlife as quickly as possible with as little pain as possible. Unfortunately, he never got any credit for this: it went to the operator of his machine, Guilliam.[75] And, instead of the device being called after al-Homsi; it took its name after Guilliam. Even to this day do I feel indignant and upset at Guilliam's treachery. Al-Homsi, on the other hand, never cared for the *guillotine* a bit. It was just his little and insignificant contribution to science.[76] When I would express my indignation that he deserved credit for such an invention, he shook his head and brushed me away saying:

'My son, knowledge is what matters, not my name.'

He cared not for titles, praise or credit and always adopted a nonchalant or stoic approach to his treachery. Instead, he concentrated at the multitudes of heads that would fall and make mathematical calculations using the circumference of the square to find out how many and how swiftly his machine could dispatch the condemned. The result was so fascinating that I even spotted him chortling as he studied the strange reaction of the severed head as it realised that it had just been severed from its body.

---

[75] The English equivalent to the name is William. [Trans.]

[76] See *The Origins of Mass Warfare and the Makings of the Atomic Bomb*, Stephen Eberhardt, London, (1998).

'What a poetic metaphor', he would exclaim enraptured, 'for the soul leaving the body!'

To return from this aside, the young bishops of the kingdom embraced the King's ideas with ease. Apart from the doctrine being clear, it no doubt empowered them in their position and station. As soon as the old order was removed or neutered, the younger bishops moved into the glorious churches of the old order. Therein, on the altars and pulpits, they began to proselytize Adolphius's doctrines to the people. They did it with such vehemence and zeal providing considerable evidences from the Holy Book that the simple people thought it a new doctrine. The populace thought the Adolphian doctrine was something very different from what they had been previously taught. This was no doubt due to the still latent strain of Arianism that was awakened within their souls. Their simple minds could not fully comprehend that it *was* actually the same doctrine but explained in a simpler manner. Consequently, they asked further questions such as: did the Son beget the Father or did the Son beget the Ghost? Did the Son come from the Father or was the Father co-equal to the Son? Why would the Eternal Father need a Son? What was the meaning of *beget*? What of the Holy Ghost? Was *three, one* or *one, three*? Were they co-equal with different essences or were they made from the same essence? How could the Eternal take on a limited numbered form? The bishops, realise that they were speaking to a simple peasant people, made up of the Visigothic and Vandal species, harangued:

'God can do anything, you dolts!'

Many a sermon was delivered by Archbishop Adolphius to elucidate on the matter, until, understanding that the people couldn't grasp the sheer simplicity of his doctrine, he developed the doctrine of *Dogma* or, as it was known later, 'The Doctrine of Blind Intelligence'. As he explains in his *Summa Adolphia*, it was based on the *mystical* and the *intangible*.[77] According to him, God was ungraspable; incomprehensible to the simple peasant mind and required that the peasant simply *believes* and did not *ask* irrelevant questions. The thinking would be done by those who understand God and could divine His will, namely the clergy.[78] It was brilliant, all the thinking was done for him! All the Frankish peasant had to do now was merely be scared that, if he *asked*, he would be excommunicated and suffer eternal damnation. Only once this theory had been developed and firmly instilled in the mind of the peasant did the questions end.

In Rome, however, the Pope did ask questions. He was quite bewildered and flustered by the whole affair. Faced, as he was, with mixed reports of the beliefs of the King and his clergy. Each one of his messengers gave a contradictory account of Adolphius's actual doctrines. The Pope reasoned thus: if the information was uncertain, how could he simply excommunicate a fellow believer, a powerful king who contributed to his monasteries and helped Christendom against the infidel? The Pope was in the business of saving, not excommunicating, after all! He did not want to condemn the king and his followers without ascertaining their exact beliefs. What resulted from the Pope's diligence, was that a steady stream of friars, notables and priests crossed the impassable Pyrenees in order to verify and confirm

---

[77] *Summa Adolphia* is now lost but extracts and references can be found in many medieval sources. [Trans.]

[78] This was very similar to the Neo-platonic conception of philosopher king. It was no wonder then, why Ibn Fudayl liked the idea. [Trans.]

these doctrines. Through this way did Spanish Christendom come closer to the rest of Western Christendom. Through this way did they mutually enrich each other in their understanding of the Divine. It is wonderful how al-Homsi played such an unwittingly fruitful role. Glory be to him!

ON OUR RETURN

We left the Kingdom of Aragon like two glorious kings, with much pomp and fanfare spent on our departure, despite us pleading with the pious king not to spend Sultan Abdullah bin Mardanish's wealth in such a superfluous way. Because we deemed it better that he spent it on the security of his nation by arming them further. Yet how foolish are kings! He scoffed at our protests and chuckled warmly and said that with al-Homsi's ingenious teachings he could make up for this extravagance within a month or two! Alas! After several weeks of feasting, we rode in to Valencia on our dignified steeds, as if we were noble men; each and everyone in the city were astounded by our mien and humble demeanour for none could recognise us in our luxurious and foreign robes of finery and thought us messengers of the great and glorious King Alfonso II, long may he reign.

We were thus given immediate access to the Sultan Abdullah bin Mardanish's presence, who recognised us for who we were: men who were seeking wisdom and did not hanker after the petty superfluous wealth of kings and princes. After talking and whispering in great length with al-Homsi and throwing numerous glances at me, I was given an opportunity to give the sultan a personal lecture. Admittedly, it was quite nerve racking at first, for I had so many lectures I wanted to present. I quickly made a mental calculation of his cranium and divided it by the hypotenuse of his nose and realised that the sultan would not be able to grasp the subtlety of my arguments. Hence I, to be safe in the knowledge that he would comprehend and perhaps even enjoy himself, gave him a private lecture on a relatively simple topic entitled: 'On the Nature of the Triangular Square World in a Parallel Universe in a Neo-Erotic Sea of Emanations'. I must say that the sultan was enthralled by the lecture and could not help but gasp in amazement at my premises, *prioris* and *axioms*. And though there were times when he did not understand the lecture, al-Homsi would step in to clarify further and present him with the tonic we had brought back from Asturias. When I finished, I was relieved to find that the sultan was duly pleased with my humble intellectual capabilities. So excited was he, so powerful was my speech, that he raised his cup and yelled:

'Give me more, you great Man of Wisdom. O philosopher, give me more!'

Both al-Homsi and I complied, for whilst al-Homsi poured the Asturian tonic into his cup, I followed on with a second lecture I had presented to the Siyasan public, entitled: 'On the Beard: A Radical Middle Way'. The sultan collapsed with delight like the drunk Hallaj.[79]

In due recognition of my considerable abilities, he became my patron and lodged me in his palace, where he began asking for my presence in his nightly gatherings. At first I refused, for I did not wish to sit amongst sycophants, poets and dancing girls; my interests laid elsewhere and were, in comparison, somewhat otherworldly. But he impressed me in attending this

---

[79]   A famous Sufi mystic who was 'drunk in God'. [Trans.]

nightly event that stopped only on Thursday night, in preparation for the Friday prayer. I was a man who hated to show bad manners to a host and rather reluctantly acquiesced, despite it going on late into the night. I soon discovered however, that his gatherings were far from what I imagined. It was filled with some of the finest intellectuals from all over the world. For example, I came across a Greek scholar from Athens, a certain Anaximander, who had demonstrated the possibility that square circles could exist and proved to me that from a certain mountain near Alicante, at a certain time, at an exact altitude it was perfectly possible to behold a square circle! The very same man showed with great accuracy the laws which he called *gravity* by means of releasing a large mallet like object on the skull of live poultry. Al-Homsi, however, was not so much interested in that, but his keen eye sight had realised that the Valencian species of poultry were the most resilient ones, to the great pleasure and joy of the Valencians.[80]

Though my nights were spent in intellectual exchanges, my days were filled with teaching. The sultan had deemed it fit that I begin a tenure at the University of Valencia. My lectures were received by the philosophers, critics and the students with applause and appreciation. For, as al-Homsi said, my lectures enthralled the imagination. As for my practical experiments, I took them to new levels. My demonstrations in the lecture hall attracted at times over five hundred students. I remember when I was demonstrating the viscose nature of Valencian faeces by heating it in sulphuric acid. The suspense was so intense that

---

[80]   See 'The Birth of Spanish Nationalism and the Civil War' in *Imagined Societies: Reflections on the Origins and the Spread of Pseudo-Erotic Nationalism*, Benedict Anderson, Princeton, (1978).

George R. Sole

it not only brought coughs and gasps from the crowd, but it even caused the women, as well as men, to faint! From these public and open lectures, I devised a classification scheme, now known as the *Fudayli ratio*, which classifies Valencian faecal matter into various strata namely: 'viscose', 'fluid', 'rock hard' 'silent', flamboyant', 'irreverent' and 'buoyant'.[81] I lay down the

---

[81] See *A Brief Discussion of the Classification of Valencian Faecal Matter Including a Brief of the Fudayli Ratio*, Michael Cook, Bradford, (1998), in which she says: 'Due to the sheer diversity of Valencian Manure and its constant refusal at being classified or defined, which means that sometimes, depending on the type of matter used, the yield in Valencia can differ greatly. This is due to (i) the phosphate content in the matter, (ii) the rate of chemical diffusion of it into the soil, (iii) rain fall, (iv) sunshine, (v) quality of the seed. For example, if the seed has been imported from the barbarian countries, it follows then that the seed will be of inferior quality. It does not matter how much rain, sun and how much of the finest grade of Valencian matter is applied, the yield will always be less due to its barbaric quality. The Fudayli ratio ranges from -23 to 256.12. When the matter is between -23 to 0 it is considered 'silent'. The phosphate and the ureic acid does not go through a process of osmosis. The matter is usually exceedingly dark and small emitting no particular smell. 'Silent' is only recommended for growing tomatoes and cucumbers, although some Valencian peasants have noticed that even rice grows well under its calming influence. This, however, is a myth brought about by the plebeian mind that is in such a state of ignorance, it cannot go beyond its horizons. When the faecal matter is between 0 to 21 it is considered 'viscose'. This is brought about usually by eating a certain kind of Andalusian mulberry or the *subbar* in great quantities. This can actually be induced by the farmer should he wish. The texture as the name suggests is viscose, it carries the trademark brown reddish colour with a yellow tint on the skin of the droppings. Looks, however, can be deceiving: though viscose on the outside, this faecal matter contains a hard core that is inflexible to the touch. In order to determine its suitability one can, if one is brave, either taste to try and get traces of the mulberry seeds or take in its scent. It should have an air of mulberry around it, with a hint of bergamot at the end. As one can guess, it is good

for all kinds of berry cultivation but its rock hard interior, along with its rich phosphate content, means that it is also perfect for truffles. It is sometimes also referred to as the 'worm hole' due to it being a particular favourite of the blue bottle. Perhaps the hardest to collect is the matter which falls between 22 and 59, it is so rare and difficult that it has been called 'fluid'. It is pure and unadulterated because of its liquid nature and has the highest phosphates. Its odour has a tinge of the Frankish - I mean, the scent is extremely malodorous. However, it is also the hardest thing to collect because it is absorbed immediately, and therefore is perfect for growing pumpkins and melons. When matter falls between 60 and 100 it is considered 'flamboyant': this kind of faeces is one of the most versatile in that it achieves a perfect balance of texture, chemical content and colour. It comes also in many different hues ranging from black to dark brown occasionally peppered poetically by red dots and white worms. One would suggest, that it is perfect for rice, legumes and fruit growing and also exporting to the Frankish nations that consider it a great delicacy. Perhaps the most specific of matter is the 'rock hard'. It ranges from 101 to 156, it is usually poor grade stuff suitable only for selling to the kingdoms in the north. Farmers have reported that for the cultivation of dates it is ideal. But this has not been confirmed by scientific research. The texture is hard, resembling a rock, an animal the excretes such matter is usually old and on the verge of death. It is recommended that the animal should be put down for humane reasons, since the rock hard matter causes havoc in the intestines of the animal and eventual death. From 157-221 it is considered 'buoyant' the matter is light and fluffy to the touch with no distinctive taste. The hue is light brown, powdery and it easily crumbles. It is perfect for cherries and flowers, providing the minerals, especially calcium and phosphates, that they need. If the matter falls between 222 and 256.12 it is considered 'irreverent': this is the rarest variety and a pleasure to behold and find. It is so rare that it appears only when it wants to appear, hence the name irreverent, it can come in many shapes and sizes usually it is a globule of light red colour, its odour or scent being exceedingly overpowering. This is due to the high sugar content in the matter, hence it will be accompanied by many flies that proliferate around it. This kind of faecal matter should only be used for the royal gardens, since they demand only the best.'

ratio, the colour and the exact chemical conditions in order for future scientists to classify faecal matter.[82] But the reader should not accuse me merely of showmanship, for I provided up to twelve volumes of empirical data on the subject. And although those were perhaps the most beneficial contributions that I made to Valencian society, my own personal favourite, was the philosophical treatise and demonstration that proved that 'nothing was really *Real*, nothing *existed* and yet everything *existed*, nothing was *Right* and yet everything was right'. I proved this theory by using the river Duero as the prime example and showed to my students conclusively that it was not really *Real*.[83]

CONCERNING THE LAST AGE OF AL-HOMSI

Realise that although the soul lives forever in the ephemerally complex universe, our life on this earth is numbered. It is when we die that we see things for what they really are, for we are like men

---

[82] See *Al-Homsi: Panoptic Pseudo-Cogencies,* F. Leavis, Oxford, (1969). The professor is somewhat elitist with this theory. This is a familiar debate in Britain and indeed Europe vis-à-vis the debate between the Utilitarian and the Romantic schools. Leavis has tried to incorporate philosophy, literature and science into a broader more Germanic understanding of science as *Wissenschaft* that should eventually lead to a sort of *blitzkrieg*.

[83] The proposition has been mistaken, as Kant has shown in his *Critique of Pure Reason (1781)*, however the principle seems sound. In connection to this theory, many students of philosophy in Valencia would jump off the bridge either to prove or disprove that the river existed. The number of deaths in Valencia was such that, it was said, the Duero burst its banks in protest. However, the truth was that the Sultan Mardanish redirected it in order for the practice to end. The sultan's redirecting of the river meant that, up to the present day, it remains a park used by Valencians for recreation.

tied to a cave where we see mere shadows on the outside, thinking that is the *Reality*. But when we have died we see the truth for what it really is; life was merely a parallel universe of illusory trigonometric shapes that signified nothing. Some of us however, have managed to free ourselves from these chains that bind humanity in this universe and see the world and the cosmos in its true techni-trigonometric insulated loft colours and try desperately, as it were, to inform and teach. Alas! No one believes us. And sometimes, in our endeavours, you meet your downfall simply because you see what other men cannot see. Death is the universal leveller for most of us, for when we descend into the earth, every man, woman and child sees the *Truth*.

I have realised that al-Homsi's message was at times impossible to comprehend. Very few men were brave enough to face up to themselves and investigate whether his words were really *Truth*. For you will find, dear reader, that most men are pitiful cowards who cannot be objective and remove their prejudices and look at his words in the cold light of their intellect. Sometimes an individual might manage to do so, but the consequences of his discovery and all that the discovery entails, the changes, the hardship, the difficulties mean that he buries himself in the sands of obscurity and hopes that the seeds of doubt do not afflict them. He resorts to follow his predecessors, assuming that they were correct, although perhaps they were people who lacked intellect. These persons, dear reader are the most pitiful persons; the cowards of this world who know and yet choose to put their intellect on hold. They choose to be ignorant or, as the great ascetic poet said, 'those who possess reason but no religion or religion but no reason.'[84]

---

[84]   Abu l-ʿalaʾ al-Maʿarri (d. 1057), a poet, freethinker who was born in Maʿarrah, Syria, lived in Aleppo and Baghdad [Trans.].

For several years, I studied at the feet of my master. It became such that not a day would go by without spending time together. He would wake up and inquire about me. I would wake up and see to it that his breakfast was prepared. I would wear robes that pleased his eye. He in turn would wear perfume only in order that it pleased me. I would say *bandora* and he would say *tamatim*.[85] He would drink and I would serve. I would eat and he would serve. In the baths, he would rub my back while I would rub his front. There was not a single mental nor physical need that I could not somehow cater for and, likewise, there was nothing that cooled my eye more than watching him twist his mustachio, place his only hand on my neck and give me an affectionate hug before he began the lesson of the day.

Realise that although al-Homsi's repute, and consequently mine, became famous throughout the province and outside the civilised world, there was no shortage of envy. Many a well-wisher was happy when we were invited to travel to the imperial cities of Marrakech and Fez to deliver lectures in their institutes. But there were also many whose faces became black with secret hatreds when they heard the same news. Nevertheless, watching this descendant of Socrates walk in the markets of Valencia, devouring countless apples, philosophizing with the fruit seller whether the ones he ate were actually real; you would never think he was plagued by their envious glances. It was a sight to behold! And it was envy that eventually led to my master's departure.

---

[85] The expression is difficult here for it is a play on words, but both mean tomato. This is mere rhetorical flourish and one suspects that Ibn Fudayl is showing off his literary skills. [Trans.].

ON HIS DEMISE

I can only say that my intimate liaison with him meant that I was witness to some of the most influential works that the civilised world has ever seen. Over the years that I studied under him his work rate was magnificent, especially after I bought the villa that served as a lyceum for him, a short distance away from Valencia. On my insistence, I installed him there where he could continue his ruminations in the olive groves of peace and serenity. And like that Persian mathematician[86] who turned to the Daughter of the Vine, likewise al-Homsi, fuelled by the vine and receiving the daughters of Valencia made a detailed commentary on Ibn Sina's *The Epistle of the Bird*[87] and *The Epistle of Love.*[88] He wrote a fifteen-volume, illuminating commentary on Aristotle's *Analytica Posteriora.*[89] He wrote his major works on ethics, the three-volume book, *My Opinion of the Virtuous City;* his small tract 'An Illumination on Liber de Causis'. He produced

---

[86] Ibn Fudayl is making a reference to Omar al-Khayyam of Nishapur (d.1123) who, in his *Rubaiyaat,* despairs at humanity and turns to 'the Daughter of the Vine'. [Trans.] See also *The Rubaiyyat of Omar Khayyam*, Edward Fitzgerald (trans.), London, (1868).

[87] A metaphor for 'woman' which has entered the English language and is still extant amongst the lower-class males in London, see the significance of *Al-Homsi, Avicenna in the Post-Natal Semiotics of Cockney Rhyming Slang,* Peter Byrd, Barking, (1991).

[88] See *The Poetics of Avicenna's Homo-Eroticism in the Oriental Mindset*, F. Rosenthel, Old American Oriental Society, (1978).

[89] Ibn Rushd (d.1198) made a similar commentary on the works of Aristotle which brought leading scholars to suspect that al-Homsi was a former student of Ibn Rushd, not only because al-Homsi's explanation has parallels with Ibn Rushd, but also because his refutation of Ibn Rushd was of such a personal nature.

An Explanation on Ibn Bajjah's Conduct of the Solitary[90] and a
refutation of Razi's work. He also made an academic refutation
on Ibn Rushd's *The Incoherence of the Incoherence*,[91] but perhaps
his magnum opus must be the definitive work on Aristotelian
Neo-platonic peripateticism, known amongst his students as
Posteriora Analytica.[92] This research involved us both in deep
philosophical struggles that tore us apart not only mentally but
also physically. Up to this day, as a result of his researches, do I
walk funny; it is unmistakably as a result of that most painful
but necessary book of his, *Posteriora Analytica*. For he explored
every orifice of thought, in order to give the world a detailed
description of our findings and a glance into the unknown
frontier of the parallel universe. I myself had the great fortune to
produce the now famous tract, common in even the most basic
book markets or copyists' shelves, that teaches the soul how to
deal with this capricious universe.[93] It was at the height of his
fame when everyone was running around discussing the book
that my whole world shook.

It pains me greatly to recall those times, but I shall now
relate to you the details of his demise. Some say that it was an
assassin from the East, sent by al-Khurasani himself; others
have said that it was one of the disgruntled Short Beardists,

---

[90]   Known in Arabic as *Tadbir al Mutawahhid*. [Trans.]

[91]   See *L'Ideologie Arabe*, Fernando Braudel, Paris, (1962). Professor
       Braudel demonstrates clearly the roots of Arab violence and discord
       that are dormant in Arab thought, which has only now reached its
       full flower.

[92]   See for further elucidation *The Being of Nothingness*, Jurgen Shapiro,
       Cambridge, (1976).

[93]   Believed to be *On the Soul* (now lost). Wrongly attributed, in my
       opinion, to Ibn Tufayl (d.1185).

others venture it was one of his own students who was so jealous of our intimacy that he reeked his vengeance on the object of his love. The perpetrators could have been many in this heinous crime.

The province of Valencia had received that most absurd book, *On the Absolute Absurdity of the Absurd*, written by that man from Khurasan, Abu Firas bin Ghassani.[94] Al-Homsi had heard from

---

[94]   Abu Firas bin Ghassani (d.1189), originally from the Arab tribe of Ghassasina, but his forefathers had emigrated to Khurasan, central Asia. He was an intellectual and a poet and is said to have studied at the Nizamiya. He made a detailed refutation on Simon Maimonides's *A Guide to the Perplexed*, known as *On the Absolute Absurdity of the Absurd*. The refutation was so perplexing that his student at-Taymi (d. 1213) made a commentary known as *The Clarification of the Perplexing*, which was further explained by Ahmad al-Seljuqi (d.1299). The work however, remained incomplete due to the death of Seljuqi. *The Clarification*, as it had become known, was then taken to Baghdad whereby it was commented upon by Ahmad as-Sindi (d.1356). As-Sindi discovered great errors in the Aristotelian logic of the work and sent it to Sind where an additional explanation was made by the great Sheikh al-Bengali (d. 1399), who introduced into it the mathematical accuracy of his native land. Unfortunately, however, the mathematics, although accurate, were so complex that the scholars were unable to fully comprehend it. Thus, one of the students of al-Bengali took it to the fledgling state of Usman, where it was further annotated by Ottoman scholars over the following centuries. By the 17th century, there had been exactly three hundred additions to *The Clarification*. Through the increasing intercourse between East and West, it found its way into Germany and France, where the Enlightenment philosophers made an attempt to solve the inconsistencies. The fruits of their work on this text have reached various degrees of success, John Stuart Mill failing abysmally with his treatise *On Liberty*, which completely misses the point; and Kant's *Critique of Pure Reason* (1781) seems to come closer to the matter. For a discussion of this subject see *Perplexing Perplexities in the Hegelian Paradigm*, Arthur Kropotkin, London, (1989) and also *Lord of the Rings: A Homo-erotic Reading*, Arthur Kropotkin, London, (2007).

many of his friends that the book was causing quite a stir in most of the civilised world. Baghdad, Damascus, Isfahan and many other cities were perusing and discussing the treatise. As a consequence, he could not wait for those leather-bound tomes to arrive on these beautiful shores. He was so excited that when they arrived, he read the five-volume book within three days and three nights. Once he finished, however, the great sheikh's mood was sombre and dark. He walked around his home shouting in a kind of delirium:

'This is absurd! It's simply absurd!'

I did not understand his mood. I tried to reach out to my master, hoping with my soothing words to comfort him. But he was indignant; shaking his fist he would shout: 'But this is absurd! Does this fellow think he is Anaximander or Xenophon?'

The book had soured him. It played on his mind. Only after a week, could he bring himself to speak fully on the subject. We were sitting in the study and he began to speak against the author and the book. For two hours he made a complete rebuttal of the arguments. So convincing were those arguments that I, before even reading the first page, was convinced of its ridiculous nature and its intellectual falsehood.

The book also made quite a stir in the province of Valencia. There were some disturbances in Siyasa; it caused an uproar in Murcia. In the weeks that followed, more and more Valencians became familiar with this heretical book that is even now being outrageously copied by scribes at the book market. It is only natural that the grand old sheikh should worry. He worried how these ideas would affect the minds of the impressionable people. Watching the ignorant purchase the book, he began to worry, how could these dangerous ideas be refuted?

'Civilisation as we know it, nay, the World as we know it will perish! To arms! To arms!'

He would say languishing on his *diwan*.

It was down to me to make the sultan aware of the dangerous nature of such a book. But it seemed that even he had come under its noxious putrid influence. Many intellectuals, too, were worried by the book, and therefore it was decided that the University of Valencia should host a lecture, delivered by al-Homsi, on the controversial book. He worked furiously for several days and nights without sleep to prepare that lecture.

Know that most of the city of Valencia and many scholars from Murcia attended the lecture. Tents and camps were set up the previous day in expectation of the crowds attending the lecture. The whole city seemed to have a festive atmosphere. There were jugglers, fire eaters, and other riff raff entertainers in every corner, whilst the *souqs* made a booming trade.

The lecture convened after the evening prayer. The hall at the university was filled with all kinds of people. His lecture began in a most verbose and skillful way. The body of the lecture consisted on a point by point rebuttal of al-Khurasani's book. He called the argument 'Milesian', which was highly amusing and I chortled so loudly that I was remonstrated for it. He proved its fallacy with the logic of Anaximander. The subject was so risible that many a fellow sat smirking throughout the lecture. Alas! The philosopher was tragically prevented from drawing a conclusion to his lecture.[95] For an assassin, disguised

---

[95] P456, *Moorish Spain*, R. Fletcher. The inability to conclude the lecture actually resulted in the downfall of the Sultanate of Valencia. Christian sources have noted that, when Valencia was finally

as a student, suddenly emerged from the crowd and dispatched him to the parallel utopia with the corner of a voluminous book he had concealed under his robes. The book lodged itself firmly in al-Homsi's cranium. The sheikh, with the book stuck in his head, tottered for a while; I rushed towards my master with tears in my eyes, trying to support the fall, but I was unable to hold his great weight and he fell down, martyred. I, underneath, had to be dragged out nearly dying of asphyxiation. A shriek went out across the hall. Men realised that al-Homsi was mortally wounded. They seized the assassin, as he tried to make his escape. The mob began beating him mercilessly until he expired. Meanwhile, as al-Homsi lay there in the throes of death, he absolutely forbade the crowd from hurting the assailant until he had recovered. But alas! It was too late. I saw al-Homsi's eyes see '*the unveiling*', as if he had realised that the parallel of the universe was insulated. He placed a passionate kiss on my lips and expired. We buried him within several hours and the mantle of the work fell on me.

Many years have passed now. I try to walk in his footsteps, I try to reinvigorate this province with his ideas. I ask questions, but the luster is no longer there. Some days I succeed, other days I fail. Some days I write melancholic poetry, reminiscing about days gone by and other days none. No one seems to understand me. I lecture and write on inconsequential subjects. Food has no taste, I am plagued with incessant migraines. I write this epistle

---

recovered from the Moors, the city could not make a unified resistance because they had not fully agreed on what the conclusion to the lecture was. It meant, naturally enough, that the Christian army could over run the city since the city was still discussing the exact meaning of what 'absurd' meant.

or treatise on his life, in the hope that his teachings and mine will somehow change and help the reader to reach the truth of the matter. May he search and question everything he holds dear to himself. For, after all, what was the point of al-Homsi's life if it cannot make a change in yours? If you, O reader, cannot see what then was his life worth?

> *O al-Homsi, you fertilising turd!*
> *My soil has become dry and barren.*
> *O al-Homsi, fertilise and return!*
> *You are my grazing bearded herd!*

Bibliography

ORIENTAL SOURCES

Al-'Ilm al-Sadid fi Mufradat al-Kalb, The Accurate Science of the Synonyms of the Dog, by Dr Rabie bin al-Kalb bin al-Kulayb bin al-Kilaab bin al-Jahsh, (Oxford), 2001.

Jihad al-Fannan al-'Azeem li-Rembrandt, Francois Boutfliqa Arkon, Beit Jabri, (1989).

Al-Wadih fee Balagha, Muhammad Ashraf Ali, Calcutta, (1896).

Al-Hikma lil-Daalin, Muhammad Ayyub Darwish, Cairo, (1923).

Sharh al-Wadih fee Takri' al-Homsi, Abu Jamil al-Badawi, Cairo, (1923).

Al-Munkidh min ad-Dalala, Abu Hamid al-Ghazzali, Beiruti, (1987).

Ibn Khallikan's Biographical Dictionary, Lane, (1889).

Sirr min al-Asrar fi Obodiyaa Rabbi il-Alameen, Majd ed-Deen as-Siyaasi al-Andalusi, translated by Eduard du-Lavatoire, Cairo, (1978).

Al-'Alama al-Andalusi fii 'Asr Muluk at-Tawa'if, Abdullah Majdi, Cairo, (1967).

Tarikh al-Harb bayna al-Juwayriya wa al-Badawiya fee Balancia ithna Mulk al-Muwahideen', Al-Kindi, Cairo, (1876).

OCCIDENTAL SOURCES

Jermaine Nigel, *The End of Patriarchy: How Arab Lexicographers Implemented EU Equality Directives in the Middle Ages: A Post-Colonial Neo-Conservative Reading,* Tusk, (2011).

Arabic Panegyric Poetry, Nabil Alam, Beirut, (1978).

Oriental Scholasticism, Market Economics: A Marxist Approach, M. Amis, Columbia, (2002).

Imagined Societies: Reflections on the Origins and the Spread of Pseudo-Erotic Nationalisms, Benedict Anderson, Princeton, (1978).

Al-Homsi, Avicenna in the Post-Natal Semiotics of Cockney Rhyming Slang, Peter Byrd, Barking, (1991).

On Liberty, Isaiah Berlin, Pinguin, (1967).

L'Ideologie Arabe, Fernando Braudel, Paris, (1962).

A Brief Discussion of the Classification of Valencian Faecal Matter in Which a Brief of the Fudayli Ratio, Micahel Cook, Bradford, (1998).

Islamic Theology and Oriental Hedonism, Patricia Crowe, Abacus, (2007).

Philosophes, Oriental Revolutionary Intellectual Antagonist and the Seeds of the French Revolution, R. Darntan, Vichy, (1992).

Short Beardista Inspirations, Che Guevara and the Origins of the Iraq War, Frank Deutscher, Boston, (2006).

Do Androids Dream of Electric Sheep?, Philip K. Dick, Viagra, (1978).

Al-Badawi, An Oriental Precursor to Newtonian and Einsteinian World, R. Dworkins, Vintage, (2005).

The Origins of Mass Warfare and the Makings of the Atomic Bomb, Stephen Eberhardt, London, (1998).

Moorish Spain, R. Fletcher, Phoenix, (1998).

Post-Modernity in Medieval Spain, R. S. Fletcher, Atticus, (1989).

Growth of Rembrandt's Spiritual Crisis, R. Fuller, Phoenix, (1976).

The Rubaiyyat of Omar Khayyam, Edward Fitzgerald (trans.), London, (1868).

A History of the Church, B. Graham, SMC, (1998).

Tolstoy's War and Peace a Long Beard Revolution or a Call for Feminist Revolution?, Jenny Greer, Oxford, (1976).

The History of the War Between the Juwayries and the Badawis in Valencia During the Kingship of the Almohads, H.A.R. Gibb, Oxford, (1936).

Abdullah bin Mardanish, Exemplar Oriental Despot, Gieves el-Rey, Santiago, (1980).

Death in the Afternoon, E. Hemingway, Garnet, (1934).

The Party of the Siyasan Beards: The Origins of Western Democratic System and Revolution, J. Hennessy, Longchamp, (2007).

A comparison of the Moghul Invasions, and the Great Damascene Riots of the Ayyubid Age: Numbers and Casualty: A Statistical Survey, P. M. Hult, Everywoman, (1980).

Perplexing Perplexities in the Hegelian Paradigm, Arthur Kropotkin, London, (1989).

Lord of the Rings: A Homoerotic Reading, Arthur Kropotkin, (2007).

Al-Homsi: Panoptic Pseudo-Cogencies, F. Leavis, Oxford, (1969).

Siyasa: A Study in Freedom, Bernford Lewes, Paramount (2007).

The Political Spectrum of the Beard and its History, Gregor Mandel, Teshcen, (1998).

An Introduction to Galileo Galilei's Works and Influences, R. Mandeblum, Scientifica, (1967).

The History of the English Language, Justin McCarthur, University of Texas, (1978).

The Evolution of the Horse Cart and American Frontier Expansion, Robert McDermot, Teshcen, (1978).

Oriental Undertones in Clauswitz and American Modern Statecraft, William Oppenheimer, Chicago, (1999).

Il Coglione di al-Homsi, Caterina Pinto, Napoli, (1999).

Valencian Manure, Globalisation and the Shaping of Western Europe, Caterina Pinto, Napoli, (1988).

Viva l'Europa, Viva l' Occidente, Donna Prodi, Il Calamaio, (1999).

Oriental Paradigms in Western Scientific Study, Karl Popper, Oxford, (1956).

Theory of Short Beard Justice, Justin Rawls, Atticus, (1987).

The Great Philosophers, R. Scrutom, Delphi, (1998).

The Being of Nothingness, Jurgen Shapiro, Cambridge, (1976).

Origins of Spanish Bullfighting, Fernando Testarossa, Madrid, (1999).

Frankish Culture in Southern Italy, Valentina Viene, Neptune, (1989).

The Evolution of Homsian Philosophical Thought, Albert Webster, Chicago, (2005).

ARTICLES AND JOURNALS

'Al-Halabi's Jurisprudence and Development of Prussian Legal Theory', Oliver Shact, *Bulletin of School of Oriental and African Studies* (*BSOAS*), (1934).

Origins of the Marxist Leninism, Igor Abrahamovich, Pravda, issue 34567, October 15, (1923).

'Origins of Masonic Symbolism and Ritual', Jay H. Berluscone, *BSOAS*, (1945).

'The Roots of al-Gore's Oriental Environmentalism', David Brooks, *BSOAS*, (2007).

Oriental scholasticism in Occidental Spain, Patricia Crowe, *Journal of American Orientalists*, (1986).

'Hegel, al-Halabi, and Houris in clashes of thought in Abbasid Christo-Judean legal theory', *BSOAS*, (2001).

'Al-Halabi, jurisprudence and development of Prussian legal theory', *BSOAS*, (1934).

The Bedouin: An Anthropological Study, Jay Witherspoon Larkin, Chattilion, (1999).

'On the Free Will of Goats', H. Malik, *BSOAS*, (2003).

'Dostoyevsky's Gnosticism: Explaining the Square Circle, a Marxist Theism under the Lens of the Gramscian Agnostics Challenge', Arthur Probotsky, *Philosophy Quarterly*, (1989).

The Poetics of Avicenna's Homo-Eroticism in the Oriental Mindset, F. Rosenthel, Old American Oriental Society, (1978).

'Foucault, Kafka, The Da Vinci Code, Arab Masculinity and Female Bisexuality: A Deconstructionist Reading', *Journal for Arab Understanding* (JFAU), Haifa, (2003).

'Oriental Barbarism in Post-Neo Colonial Arab Women's Literature', Valentina Viene, *BSOAS*, (2002).

'A Post Marxist Oriental Text in a Neo-Hegelian Italy under the Medici Family: A Deconstructionist Feminist Critique', Francois Wilbert, *Anthropological Quarterly*, issue 1, (1978).
The Times, issue 2789, Jan 25 1989.